Wait for Me,
Michael

Other Books by Mary Stolz

by MARY STOLZ

Wait for Me, Michael

HARPER & BROTHERS
Publishers NEW YORK

For Tom

Wait for Me,
Michael

CHAPTER ONE

In the town where I grew up, a stranger was like early spring
—that is, not completely exceptional, but always noteworthy.
You'd hear scraps of conversation: "He's staying at Mrs.
Miles'," . . . ". . . a writer of some kind, a reporter or something," . . . "Mr. Northrup says he has two suitcases and a
typewriter and his ticket is from New York City. One-way
ticket, Mr. Northrup says. . . ." Mr. Northrup, Cousin Jim to
me, was the baggagemaster at the depot, news of arrivals
flowing from him in nice detail. You'd know without asking
that such references were to a newcomer. I mean, in a larger
town such sentences heard in passing would have no significance.

It was in the drugstore, the summer I was fifteen, that I
heard the above words. I don't remember who was talking.
I do remember (because I thought it over later, when every

1

detail had meaning) that I turned away without inquiring, bought the tooth paste or whatever it was, and idled on home. I knew I'd see the stranger, because I was Anny Miles, daughter of the Mrs. Miles they'd been talking about. My mother kept the nicest boarding house in town. Spool beds and rag rugs and the whitest curtains . . . nothing was ever clean enough for my mother, and she could also cook. We had a small, tasteful *Tourists* sign hanging on a standard at the edge of the walk, but since tourists almost never toured in our community, it didn't have much meaning, and our guests were usually townspeople. That summer we had a Mrs. Halley, who'd moved in with us when her son got married, and a Mr. Beard, who'd been there for a couple of years.

So, I thought, running a stick along the iron fence in front of the Thaxter property, now maybe I can get a couple of cottons. I hadn't had a new dress since I was thirteen. Everything I owned was let down and looked it. A couple of dresses that fit, I dreamed, and maybe a real copy of *Wuthering Heights*. I was a reader, the sort who'd read anything— classics, movie magazines, can labels—and mostly I went to the library or bought paper books. Once in a while I got myself a special book in proper hard covers, but with money so scarce and only two steady boarders, I hadn't added anything since *The Tale of Two Cities* the preceding fall.

A pink dress and a yellow one, I thought, and maybe *Gone with the Wind*.

Madge Thaxter, my age, boy-crazy, silly, appeared at her gate and said, "*Will* you stop doing that! You grate on my nerves something frightful."

I tried to think of something crushing to say, and couldn't,

2

so dropped the stick and shrugged elaborately. "Too, too sorry," I said, and started off.

"Hold on," Madge said, hurrying after me. "What's your rush, Anny?"

I looked at her suspiciously. Madge and I were no particular friends. She had so much more money, nerve, and self-assurance than seemed ever within my reach. And she looked about seventeen. I didn't. People said, "Isn't she young for her age?" when they thought I couldn't hear, and what they meant was I had no figure and would look even younger, like a kid dressing up, if I wore lipstick and high heels. Madge wore both, when she wanted to, and looked as if she'd been doing it for years. She could also, when she wanted to, be disarmingly friendly, and I was not proof against that. So I didn't dislike her, I was simply uneasy with her. She made me feel gawky, and in her presence I always suspected that there were things I was missing in life.

Usually I didn't feel that way at all.

I liked school. There was so much I wanted to read that a lifetime wasn't going to suffice. And I adored my mother. I placed little reliance on life, but was almost unaware of that, so much did I rely on my mother.

Only, of late, unbidden intimations would reach me that soon I'd be required, like it or no, to confess the books and Mother were part of life and not the sum. I would be obliged, in other words, to do some living of my own. It was people like Madge, already hard at it, who reminded me.

"Who's the dreamy fellow at your house?" she said quite directly because subtlety was lost on me at that time. "What's his name, for heaven's sakes?"

3

"Whose name, for heaven's sakes?" I said.

I did not connect her description with that of the people in the drugstore. In fact, I'd forgotten the conversation in the drugstore and had to be reminded that a stranger had come to town. I'd been thinking so hard about cottons and *Wuthering Heights* that the possible provider of them had slipped my awareness.

"The name, dear, of the glorious stranger in our midst."

"How should I know what his name is?" I said, a bit crossly. "Why should I know anything about him?"

"Well, after all, he's going to *live* at your house."

She sounded envious, and I thought I should in some way be able to press the advantage, but since I couldn't think how, merely said, "I haven't been home since this morning. All I know is what I heard in the drugstore."

"What did you hear?"

"Oh, for heaven's *sakes*, Madge. I heard he was there, that's all. That he has a typewriter. Cousin Jim says he came in on a one-way ticket, so he must have holes in his head or some other way to get out of town. And that's all I know."

"Maybe he's going to settle here," Madge said with a sigh. I didn't answer. "Don't you like boys at all?" she asked me abruptly.

"Boys? I thought this was a man."

"A boy-man," she said dotingly, dwellingly. "A gorgeous creature betwixt and between. *Wait* until you see him."

"I can wait," I said, out of patience.

I didn't like or not like boys. Or boy-men, for that matter. They had no place in my life at all. Not real ones, that was. I had been in love. I had been, I thought to myself, more

4

taken and shaken and stunned by love than Madge Thaxter could ever conceive of being. But my unequaled, unattainable loves were all either dead or unreal.

I adored, at that time, Sydney Carton, the passionate hero of *A Tale of Two Cities.* Oh, if I had been with him, that colorless Lucie Manette would never have blinded him to his own great worth, and her stuffy husband would have taken his own place in the tumbril, and I would have *loved* him so. I'd have smoothed his raffish clothes, and gentled his wild heart, and—and—oh, loved him, loved him.

So it had been with Keats, whose mincing, faithless Fanny Brawne I would have utterly outshone, and with Heathcliffe (though I had more trouble dismissing Kathy and had to resort, at length, to simply ignoring her) and Rhett Butler, and Rupert Brooke, whom I loved not for his poetry, nor for his character—I'd never discovered that he had any—but simply for his face, and Lancelot. The list was not endless, but it was impressive and romantic.

Until this summer the thought of my never-named adored ones made me superior to Madge and girls like her. Now I was finding them less and less a protection. When Madge turned her bright little face to mine and said, "Ooo, he's *adorable*, Anny," about a real live person, Sydney Carton, though I strove desperately to keep him blazing before my inward vision, wavered, and somehow diminished. He threatened to become a man in a book, in a way he hadn't done even six months before. I was being propelled out of my castle-strewn landscape of love and dreams into a hard-featured, unwelcoming world where every prospect terrified and only I was strange. Whether it was Madge or age that was doing this to me seemed unimportant beside the fearful fact that it was happening at all.

It now appeared that in pursuit of some solid and desirable flesh she was going to follow me right into my living room. The last time she'd been in it was at my eighth birthday party, but she swung along beside me as though we were inseparable, and what else would she do but walk me home, and I couldn't think of any way to get rid of her. I wasn't even sure I wanted to. If I had to leave the safe and beautiful world of Keats and Carton, it would be desirable to have an old acquaintance like Madge in the land of the living realities. *In other words, high school.* We stopped in front of my house, and I tried to see it through Madge's eyes. Then I wished I hadn't. What I saw was a yellow clapboard building about fifty years old with a long front porch and stained-glass panels on either side of the door. There was a wisteria vine at one end of the porch with branches thick as my wrist and leaves as dense as a wall. A rocker and two fanback wicker chairs seemed, in my mind, to cry out "Boarders," even if the sign in front had not. It looks, I thought, passed by and downcast, a place that's come low in the world and no longer attempts to conceal the fact.

Normally, I didn't notice the outside of the house enough to deplore it, but with Madge beside me I was ashamed. I was also ashamed of being so, and blamed Madge for the whole situation.

"Do you want to come in?" I asked grudgingly.

"Try to keep me out."

I didn't know whether such self-confidence was justified, even in her, but still a friend at court was a friend at court, and I was not in a position to be choosey. "Come along, then," I said, and was glad to take her inside, where everything was as bright as color and polish could make it.

Mother was in the kitchen, elbows on the table, feet curled around the chair rungs, consulting a cookbook. She looked sweet, and pretty, and young. She glanced up when we came in, ran a hand through her brown hair, and said, "Hi, girls," as if I brought friends home every day. But I knew she was delighted to have me come in accompanied. She was far more anxious than I was for me to have friends. "Have some brownies." There were two pans of them, still warm, on the sideboard.

"You mean he likes something so complicated you have to look it up?" I asked, indicating the cookbook.

Mother made it a habit to ask a new boarder, no matter how brief the visit, what he especially liked to eat. Usually she'd cook it. She called this "building good will." Mother was a castle builder, like me, but a rather more practical architect. Her dreams concerned themselves with a little inn she might one day run. We used to talk about it a lot. We knew just how it was going to look—pure New England and rambly. We knew how we'd word our advertisements in the big city newspapers. We knew just how people would come from the four corners of the world (anyway, from as far as Boston or Bangor) to put up at Miles's Country Inn. ("My dear, it's fabulous, and you won't believe it till you've *been* there.")

We knew just the place we wanted. An old farmhouse on the other end of town, farther from the highway than we were now ("An inn is not like a tourist house," Mother

7

would tell me. "You *want* an inn to be out of the way.") and surrounded by five acres of lovely meadows and trees. We called it The House and had saved some fraction of the purchase price. A miniscule fraction. Meanwhile, Mother built good will with her lemon polish and wax, her bowls of flowers, her shining windows, her "What would you especially like tonight for dinner?"

"And I'd like to tell you," she said to me now, triumphantly, "it's beginning to pay off."

"The cooking?" I said, after a moment's thought. She had a sometimes flattering, sometimes maddening, way of starting a conversation mid-thought and assuming you'd make the jump to where she was.

"Naturally the cooking," she said. "Isn't that what we were talking about? Well, *he's* here—did you know we have a roomer, a new one, he just got into town today?" I nodded, and she went on with satisfaction, "*He's* here because his uncle—do you remember that man last fall, that Mr. Vye, who strayed off the road in the thunderstorm and woke us up in the middle of the night and stayed all weekend because he liked my cooking so much? Remember him?" I nodded again. "*Well*," she said, and was by now simply sparkling, "*he's* here—the one upstairs—because of his uncle. Mr. Vye was his uncle. Still is, of course." She stopped, waiting for me to exclaim. We'd both forgotten Madge, who was quietly eating the brownies.

"You mean we got a recommendation?" I exclaimed.

"Well, I suppose we've had others," my mother was going on airily, "but just didn't know about it. I suppose that's perfectly true. However, *this* one—" She stopped and looked

8

at Madge with alarm. "Marion, dear, do leave some. I mean, they're for dinner, and I have all these mouths to feed."

"Sorry," said Madge, and I said, "It's Madge, Mother. Madge Thaxter."

"Oh, of course," said Mother. "How forgetful of me."

She knew who Madge was, but took this funny, rather childlike way of protecting me against what she considered the indifference of my schoolmates. Mother, no reader and highly sociable, assumed that my solitary ways were imposed on me, and painful. She didn't have many friends herself, in spite of her friendliness, and it sometimes seemed to me that one could have either a boarding house or a social life but not both. Mother suffered far more from this than I did.

Her curiosity and general affection for people were so strong, however, that in a moment she had forgotten she was supposed to vindicate me and was talking to Madge quite kindly about the newcomer. Madge had missed no time getting to the point.

"What's the new boarder like, Mrs. Miles? I heard he's dreamy."

"Honestly, this *town*. You can't change your brand of soap without everybody calling up to see what you had in mind." She sounded fond and indulgent, which was not my feeling about the provincialness of our town. I despised it. But Mother was all settled, like a bee in her colony. ("Move to another hive? Why, buzz my stars, I wouldn't think of it! It'd be full of *strangers*, wouldn't it?")

She put her head to one side, considering Madge's question, and said at length, "Dreamy. That's not accurate enough. He looks as if he had his head in the clouds—a very handsome head it is, too—and could tell you what quarter the moon will be in tomorrow. But he also knows what time it is now."

My mother had this way of offering little sketches of people which completely charmed me. I looked at Madge to see if she was appreciative, but she wasn't. I decided she had no imagination, and nothing she ever did later caused me to change my mind.

"Oh, come *on*, Mrs. Miles," she said now, "you aren't really telling me a thing. I mean, what does he look like really? Tall? Short? How *old* is he?"

"About twelve," Mother said promptly. Madge looked so thwarted that she smiled and added, "Well, twenty-two or three, perhaps. But he has this—this peppy look, like a little boy with dozens of interests and all of them fascinating. So many people his age look as if they'd already been pensioned, you know?" Madge shook her head. "As if there was nothing to look forward to," my mother explained.

"Oh," said Madge. "Like my sister. She's always saying the whole world is going to be blown up and what's the use of having been born if this is what you're born to."

"It isn't only people twenty-two or three feel that way," I said, and added, "I'm not talking about me," when Mother turned her quick glance my way. "I just mean . . . well, there's a girl in my class says there's no point in studying because we're never going to live to use what we learn. And Mr. Beard. He thinks the world's going to end *very* soon. My personal opinion is that he can hardly wait."

"Poor Mr. Beard," Mother said automatically.

"Daddy says my sister is just saying those things as an excuse to spend money," Madge mused. "She says if the world

10

is going to explode, she'd rather go up with sables than securities. Of course, she doesn't have either, but she did manage to get a convertible over his practically dead body. Mrs. *Miles*, we keep getting away from the boarder. I mean, what's his name?"

"Michael Vye," Mother said. She jumped to her feet and began to rummage in the closet. "Here I am," she said, "sitting here *talking*. Anny, run down to the cold room and get me those blueberries you picked this morning. Mr. Vye will have to have muffins tonight. This Sally Lunn he likes has yeast in it, so he'll have to wait till tomorrow for it. And then you'd better start setting the table, dear."

On Thursday, when Lenore, our overworked maid-of-all-work was off, I could never decide whether to be disgruntled at everything extra there was to do (I frequently, but especially on Thursdays, felt misused and overworked myself) or relieved at not having her around. She and I, from the moment we met, did not get on. She considered me disobliging, I found her a savage bore, and Mother was always trying to keep the peace between us by putting Lenore to work at one end of the house and me at the other.

"I'll help," Madge said now. "Tell me what to do, Mrs. Miles."

Mother was surprised at the offer, but I wasn't.

Of course, she'll help, I said to myself when I was out in the garden swinging the lettuce (Mr. Vye, this Mr. Vye's uncle, had sent Mother a lettuce-swinging basket from France, and we were both inordinately fond of swinging lettuce, despite laughter from boarders and neighbors). She has a fixed point in view. She's going to hang around here until Michael

11

Vye shows. What she's going to do about it once he does is anybody's guess. Madge was brash as they come, but there was no getting around her skimpy fifteen years, even if she did contrive to look older with the help of make-up and affectation.

When I got back in the kitchen she was chopping nuts and grilling Mother at the same time. "Come on now, Mrs. Miles," she was saying in that easy-going manner that all people assumed after the briefest acquaintance with my mother, "come on—give. Is he handsome rugged or handsome wispy?"

"Rugged, oddly enough."

"Why oddly?"

Mother shrugged. "He's this playwright, see. Only he's never had a success. I always think unsuccessful writers should look sort of transparent."

"He's a little young to be called unsuccessful," Madge said sharply. "He just hasn't gotten started yet, that's all."

"Maybe you're right," Mother murmured indifferently.

A playwright? I thought. Mr. Vye, his uncle, was an undertaker. A very cultivated man, and traveled, but still an undertaker. A big, bluff, articulate man who'd landed on our doorstep by accident one stormy night and had utterly succumbed to Mother's cooking. It had been my own opinion that he'd succumbed to Mother, too, but nothing had come of it and I was glad. He stayed that weekend, and the following spring sent us the lettuce swinger. Now he'd sent us his nephew.

"A playwright?" I said. "What sort of plays?"

"I don't know, dear. I just asked after his uncle when I showed him the room and he said, 'As life is death, Uncle

12

is fine.'" She paused. "I imagine that sounds more meaningful than it actually is, but I looked as if I found it *very* meaningful and asked, naturally, what he did for a living, and he said he was writing a play, and I said I was sorry but I wasn't much of a playgoer, and perhaps he could name me some of his works—"

Madge looked pitying, and I resented and agreed with her. Most of the time my mother's lack of interest in things intellectual didn't bother me, but it did now, when it gave Madge Thaxter, an intellectual absentee if I had ever known one, an opportunity to look superior.

"Playwrights," I said too loudly, "are generally not established at the age of twenty-three, Mother. They haven't got any works to name."

"Should they call themselves playwrights, then?"

"If they're working at it, and intend to be, I don't see why they shouldn't." For the life of me I could not have told if I were defending Mother against Madge, or youthful writers against Mother. Edgily I said, "Why all this talk about someone who's going to be here for a few days and then leave, anyway? It just proves how narrow and confined we are in this town—" I broke off and started collecting silver for the dining-room table.

Mother said thoughtfully, "I actually never have understood why curiosity is supposed to be limited to small towns. I'll bet if you heard some city people talking and some country people talking there wouldn't be a thing to choose between them. I mean, if you didn't *know.*"

I did not agree. In the great cities, I knew, the talk would be of art and justice, of man's future, and his spirit. Of

13

Life's riddles. Those city people would be talking *ideas*, I said to myself, and the country people would be talking politics and personalities, and I'd be able to choose between them, all right.

"Is this Mr. Vye coming down for dinner?" I asked, counting forks.

"Well, of course," said Mother. "That's half the reason he's here. His uncle told him what a good cook I am. So nice of him."

"What's the other half?" said Madge.

"Other half?"

"Of why he's here, Mrs. Miles."

"Oh . . . well, he's writing this play, and he's stuck. So his uncle told him about this lovely little country inn—he actually called this place an inn, which I think is very kind of him—where he could have a huge attic room all to himself and be fed like a king—that's what Mr. Vye said—and finish the thing in peace and quiet."

"Well, my goodness," said Madge. "It may take him *ages*. He may be here for months and months." She seemed to be trying to comfort herself, because she was probably going to have to go home for dinner before Michael Vye showed up.

"I wouldn't know. But he's just wild about the attic. City people do seem to be," Mother said.

I stalked into the dining room, not wishing to hear another word about city people. I was deciding whether to put another leaf in the table or just squeeze Mr. Vye in between Mother and Mrs. Halley, when I heard Madge leave, and then a step in the hall, and a voice. I looked up indifferently.

14

"Mrs. Miles? Oh, hello—I'm Michael Vye."

I stared. My hands opened slowly, releasing the silver, which slid with a clatter to the table top, and there I stood, saying to myself in wonder, "So they make men like this, do they? There are real, live men . . . like this."

CHAPTER TWO

I didn't stare at him during dinner. I had no need to. He was memorized and engraved upon my inward vision. I ate a little so Mother wouldn't worry and say something that would cause people to look at me. I wanted to be invisible, completely unnoticed and unremarked. I would have liked to steal from the room and lie on my bed with the dusk gathering, and my thoughts moving stilly, solemnly to what I knew was an inevitable answer.

After years of loving phantasms, dead men, and the creations of other people's minds, I had fallen in love with someone alive and really in the world. *O brave new world,* I thought, *that has such people in't.* Miranda had not looked and loved more speedily than I. The difference being that Miranda had speedily been loved right back.

Twenty-three, I thought. Or, just possibly, twenty-two. And I am fifteen. It was a woman's sorrow I felt, and I was overwhelmed and defeated by it, the way a child is. I wanted to put my head on the table and cry. I wanted to rush out of the room and down the garden to a place where the trees formed a sort of low room, the kind of place a child goes to for comfort. But I thought, as I longed for it, that I would not be going there any more. The time comes when you desert the place at the end of the garden and leave behind you the men in books. The time comes when you are no longer in love with Sydney Carton . . .

"Anny," my mother said, and I realized she'd said it two or three times, "Anny, Mr. Beard would like some more bread."

Glad of the chance to get out of the room, even for a second, I grabbed the basket and disappeared into the kitchen.

Now, give me the strength, I prayed. Help me.

I think I meant, give me dignity, keep me from being discovered. I didn't see any chance of talking myself around this. I had read too many books not to know that people can fall in love, suddenly and forever, at a glance. What I wanted was not to be found out. I had all the pride of my years. Mother, from time to time, told me I had more. She said I took everything, especially myself, too seriously. I saw no way out of that. Life was a serious business. It seemed now that love must be its most serious problem, coming like a brigand, having to be concealed like a shameful thing.

I closed my eyes for a moment and listened to his voice,

just out there in the dining room, just on the other side of the swinging door. I couldn't hear what he was saying, only the tone, which seemed to me rich and warm.

He liked talking. I knew, as the other youngest person there, that he was taking pleasure in being the center of attention. Mr. Beard had brightened at his appearance and made some chuckly reference to thank the lord, now there's another man. Mrs. Halley, immediately smitten, had already begun to tell how disgracefully her daughter-in-law treated her. Mother liked him, of course, but Mother indiscriminately liked everybody.

I did not consider it to his credit that all these older people had looked and doted—in their way—as quickly as I had. It was rather to his discredit, especially that he seemed to be preening himself under their attention. But I had a premonition that for me his faults and virtues would be side issues. I was going to love him whole, as he was.

It was too much to face without warning, and my steps dragged as I returned, bearing the bread. Mother looked at me with concern. "Don't you feel well, dear?" she asked.

"I'm fine," I said hoarsely, making an effort to look fine.

"She and her friend," Mother said in innocent but racking betrayal, "ate too many brownies this afternoon, I'm afraid."

"You'll never lose your baby plumpness that way," Mrs. Halley twitted. Mrs. Halley was a woman who said anything that came into her head, seldom bothering to check even the most ascertainable facts. Such as, I thought, faint with anger and loathing, the readily checked one that I was skinny as a rail and hadn't any *baby* plumpness to lose.

18

Full of love and hate, I stared at the tablecloth and willed them to forget me. Which, after a while, they did.

After dinner I cleared the dishes and began to do them in a mood of foreboding and nervous joy. To be in love . . . to be in love. To think that this morning I had wakened a child, with a child's fanciful ideas of where love was to be found. Oh, I knew that I hadn't been altogether persuaded by my own notions. I'd been aware that one day I'd look up from the pages to see a flesh-and-blood man who would put Sydney Carton in his place. But I hadn't expected it to happen for years. Now, in one day—

I didn't hear him come in. I just turned, and there he was.

"Oh, say, I'm sorry," he said, and caught the plate as it slid from my grasp. "I startled you."

"No. I mean, it's all right."

"I wanted a drink of water, and your mother said it would be all right if I came in and got one."

"Of course. There's some in the refrigerator."

He perched on the edge of the table, one leg dangling, looking around as he sipped his water. I kept on washing dishes, head down, painfully searching for something to say, finding nothing.

I was glad, at least, that the kitchen presented such a nice appearance. If not I, then mine, could please him. The copper pots and molds hanging on the walls, the geraniums at the window, the bright blue bowl on the sideboard, the little tiger cat, Tabu, sitting with white paws trimly together, her great yellow eyes fixed on his face—all this, which was part of me, would give him pleasure.

"This is a wonderful kitchen," he said. "It has such a scrubbed and tended look, and then it turns around and is pretty, too."

I felt almost as happy as if he'd praised my hair, or my eyes.

"It has exactly the look of your mother," he went on thoughtfully.

A poniard went through me, of protest and pain. This was my place, too. I worked here just as hard, gave it as much thought, as my mother did. "I bought the geraniums," I said before I could stop myself. "And the cat's mine."

There was a little silence, and then he said, "They're both marvelous. I can see why Uncle liked this place so. He often talks about how your—your mother and you have made the place an inn of dreams."

"It isn't an inn," I mumbled. He'd caught on so quickly to my sudden, utterly unexpected pang of jealousy that I felt mortified and began to babble for diversion. "Not a proper inn at all, you know. We have *ideas* about an inn—pretty expensive ones, let me tell you. We have the place picked out and the décor decided and a stream of notables all queued up waiting to get at the register—" I heard myself going on and on in an arch and silly way. I felt utterly desperate, and rather overheated.

"That should be great," he said when I at length ran down. "Perhaps one day you'd show me the place you've picked out."

Steadied by his matter-of-factness, I nodded, let the water out of the sink, wiped my hands, and turned, facing him directly for almost the first time. I could only look a moment

20

and then glance away, dazzled. Let him think me highstrung, or backward, I implored. Let him think I have a tic. Anything, except that he should guess the truth.

Just as short a while ago as dinnertime I'd been searching for ways to seem more mature. I'd been considering make-up and a change in personality. I'd been wondering if I could get my mother to join me in a lie. "Anny?" I'd decided she could say. "Why, she's almost seventeen. Doesn't look it, I know. But almost *seventeen*." Of course, she would not have considered agreeing, but I'd considered asking. Now I dived back into childishness like a rabbit into his brier patch. Where else was there any safety?

I perched on a stool, toes in, and said, "Okay. Sure, if you want to. How's your uncle, Mr. Vye? We thought he was awfully nice. Did you know he sent us a lettuce swinger?"

"What's a lettuce swinger?"

"A basket that you put the wet lettuce in and then swing it dry in the garden. All French peasants swing their lettuce dry. So now we do, too."

He laughed. "Uncle's fine. He sent you his warm regards."

"Thanks. Why didn't he ever come back?" Not that I wanted him to, especially, but it was something to say.

"Now that is a mystery to me."

It isn't to me, I almost said, but this time held my tongue. It was easier to talk to him now, from my brier patch of immaturity. I could look at him as much as I wished, alarming neither him nor myself. I could talk to him without having the words gallop around in a panic and perhaps, in a panic, betray what needed to be concealed. If I were a child, he would be easy with me, he might come to like me. This way

21

I might be able to . . . stalk him. The other way I'd lose him at the start.

"Mother says you're a playwright, Mr. Vye."

"Oh, no. I said I was writing a play. There's a world of difference, Anny." He stopped, then said, "Is it all right if I call you Anny?"

"Sure. Why not?"

"Well, sometimes young ladies would rather be called by their last names."

He was certainly confident of being with a child. "No, I'd like you to," I said, and he asked me to call him Michael.

"If you aren't a playwright, Michael, what are you writing a play for?"

"Just to see." I nodded, and now he smiled. "Does that make sense to you?"

"Oh, perfect sense. How is it going?"

"I don't know. That's what I'm here to find out, having convinced myself I can't write in the city but certainly could away from it. A couple of months in your splendid attic will bear me out, or find me out."

"What do you do when you aren't writing?"

"I'll be going back to school this fall to do graduate work."

"In what?"

"Chemistry."

I was awed. I had an imprecise but intensely stirring picture—he stood at a scientifically cluttered table, looking like a doctor in a long white coat, test tube held aloft before him, dedication on his marvelous face. "That's wonderful," I sighed, and he didn't disagree.

I glanced at Tabu, who'd never stopped looking at him

since he came in. She was wearing the mask of bitter contemplation that she showed all strangers, and I hoped he wouldn't notice, but he followed my gaze and said, getting up, "That cat considers me an interloper, you know. She's been trying to stare me out of countenance."

"Oh, no. That is . . . she does it to people she doesn't know. I think she feels threatened in some way—"

He looked at me with interest, and I had a perilous, sweet feeling that we were on the brink of a real conversation, that once begun it might reveal anything, anything at all.

"She's something like me," I began riskily. "She reserves judgment so long that usually the opportunity to act on it has vanished by the time she's decided."

"Are you like that?" He sounded surprised, and no wonder.

I didn't know what to say. That, in his case, old patterns were altered, old attitudes irrelevant? That the person I could competently describe as myself was, in fact, no longer with us? I have reference to the child I was a few hours ago, I might have said, but she's gone. The seeming child who sits before you now is a fraud. I am a woman who wants you, so take care.

I said, "Most of the time—"

"Anny?" Mother called. "Anny, are you still out here?"

I was furious with her. Like that flashing jealousy of minutes before, my fury dispersed itself quickly, but I'd felt it and it shook me. Mother was poised lightly in the door wearing that expectant look she so often had—a look I used to puzzle over, trying to understand what she expected, when her life was so daily, with so little prospect of change. She had some yellow roses in her hand.

23

"These are for you," she said to Michael Vye. "Six the beetles somehow overlooked. We've been having a frightful time with beetles this summer." She smiled away his thanks, burrowed in the closet for a vase, went to the sink for water, and arched her brows.

"Best I could do," I said, referring to the condition of the sink. As I say, things were never sufficiently clean for Mother and I'd given up trying to meet her standards. I did what seemed to me an adequate job, figuring if it wasn't, she'd do it over again and perhaps enjoy the opportunity.

She got a can of cleanser, sprinkled it liberally around the sink, and scrubbed away while the odor of chlorine rose in the air, defeating the delicate scent of the roses.

"This is absolutely marvelous stuff," she told us. "Heavenly."

How can she sound so intense about a scouring powder? I wondered irritably, critical of her for something I'd always found wonderful. There was nothing unimportant in my mother's life, from floor wax to funerals, but it struck me now that if everything was equally important, then everything was equally unimportant. If you brought all this emotional energy to the scouring of the kitchen sink, would you have enough left for the real things—life, death, love?

Tabu, who did not like strange odors any more than she liked strange people, lifted her striped head and turned it suspiciously from side to side, flicked her long whiskers, and got up and walked out of the kitchen, her tail high. I wondered whether to follow her. Michael Vye was explaining the chemical behavior of scouring powder, and Mother was captivated.

Watching him watch her face, seeing the delight he was taking in her excessive delight, I felt like saying, "This isn't for you, you know. It's her general reaction to life. She finds everything, everyone, delightful."

Oh, the times are out of joint, I cried to myself, my mind in a shaming state of disorder and anarchy. So I would fall in love without delay, deliberation, or reserve with a man of unsuitable age, and immediately turn on my mother for doing what she always did, which was to charm people. What if she was too easily elated? I'd always loved it till now, finding her different, superior to all the dull people going about life as if it were a chore to be gotten through, and not a piece of lucky magic, which was what Mother seemed to find it. Even if it had been years since I'd believed her, I had been a child who found life magical—because of my mother.

I have a small mind, I told myself. If she iced cookies with the silly scouring powder, it wouldn't matter, really.

All the same, I could not remain another moment listening to Mother's laugh, looking at Michael Vye's expression of surprised felicity. I felt as I thought Tabu must have, free to watch and listen to them, but alien, suspicious, primly apart.

"I'm going upstairs," I said.

Mother looked at me closely. "Still not feeling well?" she said. "I'd have done the dishes, if you'd said anything, Anny."

"I know," I said. "No, I'm fine. Good night."

I went out before they could detain me with more questions. Mother is so sweet, so very sweet and dear. I wrote the words across my mind. Uncertain what a threnody was, I

25

thought perhaps I was caught up in one, as I kept telling myself, over and over, something I knew and believed.

"Anny! Want a game of double solitaire?"

Under the lamplight in the living room, all by herself, Mrs. Halley was shuffling her worn deck of cards. She looked squatty and crumpled and sometimes I was sorry for her because she was a victim of her own unpleasantness and even a doctor wouldn't tell her that. Tonight I wanted no part of her.

"Have to do my chores," I said. "Sorry. Why don't you ask Mr. Beard?"

"He's gone for his walk," she said peevishly. "That block-long stroll he makes such a to-do about."

"Well, I'm sorry," I said again, and went up the stairs, two at a time, to my room. I had still to turn down the beds in Mrs. Halley's and Mr. Beard's room. It was part of Mother's ideal in service. But I wasn't going to do it yet. I wondered briefly whether I should do Michael Vye's bed, too. The thought of it gave me a shock of pleasure, made me aware of the blood pulsing in my wrists.

As I looked around, undecided, confused, I caught my reflection in the bureau mirror, and moved forward slowly, leaning toward the glass to stare at my face. White under its tan, flushed on the cheekbones, starey-eyed, slightly blemished. Like a waif, sort of ageless and plain.

I walked away from the bureau and sat, knees drawn up to my chest, on the wide window seat with the sycamore just outside. I suppose I was thinking, but it was all shapeless, without meaning. Tabu appeared in the doorway, stared at

26

me severely for a moment, then relented since I was now alone, and came across the room. She leaped up lightly and butted my arm out of the way so she could get close to my side. She was the most completely one-person cat I had ever known, and she was mine. We sat there in my girlish room in silence, and after a while I began to cry, with a quiet, sprawling abandon, and no attempt to understand, or stop, the flowing easy tears. I cried about everything, putting a name to nothing.

When I was finished, I put Tabu aside, got up in a matter-of-fact way, and went into the bathroom to wash my face. Mother found me there.

"Anny," she said to my back, "don't bother to do Mr. Vye's room at night."

"Oh? Why not?" I didn't turn around.

"Well . . . I just think it will be sufficient if Lenore does it in the morning. Perhaps he'll want to work at night."

I could have asked what that had to do with turning down his bed, but didn't. Mother missed little as she flitted around, and she might not know what had happened to me this afternoon, but she knew that something had. I decided not to ask questions that might clarify things.

"Okay," I mumbled, the washcloth pressed to my face.

"Anny, turn around."

I turned slowly, and Mother put her hand up and pulled the washcloth away. I endured her perceptive blue regard for a long moment and then averted my head.

"Perhaps you have a little fever, dear," she said gently. "Why don't you go to bed? I'll do Beard and Halley." She

27

had the six yellow roses in a green glass bowl. Now she put them on the table beside my bed.

"I thought they were for Mr. Vye," I protested.

Mother lifted her shoulders a little. "People who go to bed early should have roses."

I had to smile. Every once in a while she said something that was so like herself that if it hadn't been Mother, I'd have said it was rehearsed.

"Okay," I said. "Thanks."

I didn't go to bed, though. I sat on the window seat, my little cat beside me, and looked along the walk, past the gate. Out on the street the trees were beginning to toss their branches fretfully, and a cool damp smell, like mushrooms, rose up from the earth. I watched the cars go by, and the branches wave, throwing their shadows helter-skelter across the road where the lights from the street lamps fell. I saw the windows darken in neighboring houses. I heard Mrs. Halley's clump-clump ascension of the stairs, and then Mr. Beard's tired, sad-sounding step, and after a while my mother's light one accompanied by Michael Vye's, also light and quick. They spoke for a moment on the landing, and then he went on upstairs. I heard him walk across the room above, heard the rush of water running in his bathtub.

If I tried, I could fit all those lost, dear loves to him. I could imagine he had the slovenly dash of Sydney Carton, the male splendor of Rhett Butler, the profile of Rupert Brooke, the . . . But I gave up. He was none of those. He was Michael Vye, and I didn't really know him at all. But I knew that I loved him.

It was raining when I went to bed and, for the first time in my reading life, put out the light without looking at a book. I lay curled up, Tabu in the crook of my legs, listening to the rain as it beat on the porch roof under my window. Intoxicated, terrified, I lay and refused to sleep until there was no choice and I fell headlong into dreams of loving.

CHAPTER THREE

Mornings were never easy. Not even summer mornings, when the light was well advanced at six o'clock, Mother's rising time and mine. I was nearly always tired from having read too late, and—unlike Mother—the day did not challenge me with promises of unknown pleasures.

I came out of sleep reluctantly, fighting the urge to retreat and be nothing again. Behind lay the lulling softness of dreams and darkness. Ahead were boarders and meals and un-made beds and Lenore, and it was my misfortune to think of them before I remembered that the day would also bring Mother and Tabu and a chance sometime to read. And challenge, too.

In other words, Mother woke up awake, and I woke up asleep.

School days were even harder. To go from the gentle

darkness to the cold one seemed only this side of unendurable, and though I never overslept, often I began, in desperation, to read on from where I'd left off the night before, and Mother would have to call me over and over.

The morning after Michael came I awakened quickly, but with a sense of alarm, and lay looking around, not stirring. There was something . . . something had happened—and when I remembered, I cried to sleep again.

For what, now that the characters had gone back to the books, was I to do, in love with a real live man? *If I could grow up!* If, in some quarter, at any price, I could bargain for three, even two, years. As if by an effort of body and will I could force years past me in minutes, I lay with clenched teeth and tightened fists.

A tap at the door went through me like a shock. Am I never to be let alone, never to have any peace? I wondered unreasonably, and called out, "What is it? What do you want?"

Mother came in, wearing a lime-green cotton dress, full-skirted and sprigged with little flowers. Her hair was glossy, and, despite a few streaks of aluminum gray, very pretty. Her face was almost unlined, and the blue eyes sparkled with their customary morning brightness. I recalled my own image in the mirror last night. That blemished, awkward, forlorn reflection. I did not like the comparison. I resented it deeply, and I looked at my mother as I would look at a threatening stranger.

"Something wrong?" she said. "Why are you staring at me? How do you feel?"

"You look very young," I told her.

She didn't thank me, because it hadn't been meant as

or sounded like a compliment. "I feel fine. At least the sun is out."

"At least?" she said, and hurried on, "Sorry to wake you up, but you have a dentist appointment, you know. I was just talking to Dr. Roberts. I told him you'd been leaving the retainers off, and he said probably it's all right but you'll have to be there for a checkup."

Wild horses, Mother, and Dr. Roberts combined weren't going to get those retainers back on my teeth, but I decided to let actions speak for me, and, jogging downtown on the bus to Dr. Roberts' office, I thought that perhaps I'd hit on one of those universal truths that people come to unaided. Children think to win their way by protest, argument, by hysterics, if necesssary. But the fact was, most of the time they failed to get their way, and if they did it was still through some decision or caprice of their elders. Now I had this revelation which told me that the way to get your way was to say nothing, but go ahead and take it.

Absorbed in my imperious dreams, I went past my stop and had to walk back.

Dr. Roberts poked, pried, tapped, and tested. At length he walked to the sink and washed his hands, saying over his shoulder, "Well, everything seems to be in order, Anny. You needn't wear the retainers after this."

I could have told you that, I thought, and said, "Thanks a lot, Dr. Roberts."

"Not at all. I know you're relieved. You have a fine set of teeth there, just like your mother's. See that you take care of them. And then"—he gave a snort—"you won't be in the position of the woman who just went out of here."

32

"What's her position?" I asked.

I didn't, really, care in the least about her position, but part of my plan for the enchantment of Michael Vye was to overcome my almost total indifference to what most people were doing or thinking. Clearly he found nothing too trivial to awaken his interest. He'd listened to Mrs. Halley's self-pitying complaints as if she were explaining a new law of mathematics. He'd lent an attentive ear to Mr. Beard's gentle prediction of bad weather for the remaining weeks of summer. Look how he'd reacted to Mother's happy praise of the scouring powder.

Until yesterday I could have found sympathy for none of this. I could break my heart over Jo, the crossing sweep boy, but not over Mr. Beard. I could shake my head with rueful understanding as Mrs. Adams ruined Alice's dreams, but I could only wrinkle my nose with distaste as Mrs. Halley (possibly Mrs. Adams' counterpart) whined about her daughter-in-law. But Michael Vye was kind and curious about the people around him, and I was going to be kind and curious, too, if it meant giving up books forever.

So I looked at Dr. Roberts and said, "What's her position?"

"Her boy friend bought her a set of teeth, uppers and lowers, and then when he walked out on her, took them with him."

"Huh?"

"So help me. Said he'd put three hundred dollars in them and wasn't going to leave it behind."

"Why did she give them to him? I'd have bitten him first."

"She didn't know how to refuse, poor thing."

"For goodness' sakes," I said, thinking this awful anecdote

33

was not really suitable for someone my age, so maybe I looked older than I was, after all. I shifted around, wanting to leave, aware that I didn't feel in the least kindly toward the woman. I just thought she was silly. "Are you going to help her out?"

"Help her out? I'm going to make her new teeth, if that's what you mean."

I couldn't ask if he proposed to do it free of charge, so I left after thanking him once more for allowing me to do what I'd intended to do anyway.

Outside, the sun was white-hot and shimmery. People moved slowly, as if their heels stuck to the pavement at each step, and the church bells, ringing eleven at that moment, did not seem to rise and float and fly away as they did in cool months, but toppled and fell heavily, like old pillows. There were tar bubbles in the street and a smell of tar in the air. An ice-cream wagon went by with children clinging to it like wasps, and I, suddenly apathetic with emotion and heat, turned into The Boston Spa for a limeade.

I had finished it and was reminding myself that I had marketing to do and had better get on with it, when Madge and her sister, Maureen, came in, carrying packages that looked like dresses and a hat. They bought dresses the way I bought Kleenex, and for the first time I reacted with a spasm of envy. I got up, knocking over my glass, righted it, and started out hoping not to be noticed. But the predatory sisters were not letting me, possible road to a rainbow, escape.

"Anny!" Madge shrieked. "Anny, don't go! Here we are."

"So I see."

Reluctantly I approached their table and stood, attempting

34

to look like someone on an urgent mission. The air-conditioning in The Boston Spa wasn't working too well, and it was difficult to look urgent about anything, but I blinked and tried.

"Have to get along—" I began, but Madge patted the seat beside her and inertia dragged me down.

"How are you, Anny?" Maureen said oversweetly. "How come we never see you any more?"

When did you ever see me at all, except on your way past? I wondered. Here was yet another person—two people—in whom I had to be interested despite their basic lack of interesting qualities. I began to be afraid that that sort of reaction (Mother's and Michael Vye's) had to be spontaneous if it was not to be an insupportable burden. Please, I thought, oh, please, don't let me give up soon. Maybe in time, with practice, I'll be spontaneous, too, and I'll care about the Madges and Maureens, and unknown women in Dr. Roberts' office, without trying at all.

I smiled and stared into Maureen's face, telling myself it was very pretty if you liked that reckless, faintly depraved look, and some people did.

"Oh, I stay awfully busy," I said. "What do you have there? Lots of gorgeous clothes?" The smile was now stuck on my lips and only effort would have removed it. I noticed Madge eying me curiously, but ignored her. First things first, I thought, and I've already begun with Maureen. "Your hat?" I asked her, waving an airy hand at the box.

"Oh, yes. It's luscious. I said to the salesgirl, 'But that isn't to be worn, it's to be eaten!'" She stopped, and I realized I was expected to smile. Since I was already smiling, I was obliged to laugh. "Oh, do open it up," I pealed. "Let's have a *look* at it."

Maureen was pleased to comply, and while she was busy with the string, Madge said to me, "Are you feeling all right?"

"Of course I am. What makes you ask that? Oh, what a *love* of a hat, Maureen!"

"You sound *most* peculiar," Madge insisted. "And you look peculiar, too."

"Madge, don't talk that way," Maureen said reprovingly.

But her sister's remarks had sobered me, and my somewhat tipsy smile fell away abruptly. Maybe, I thought, my head beginning to throb, these are the wrong people to start with. Can you be kindly and curious about people and jealous of them at the same time? I coveted their clothes, their look of maturity (Maureen was nineteen and I wondered if she knew how lucky she was, and decided she probably did), their self-confidence. Only yesterday, I remembered, I was planning how to use Madge as a friend at court. I was going to cultivate her and so smooth my emergence from the world of letters to that other one, the world of people my age. Now I could not have cared less.

"Listen, Anny," Madge went on, "we're going to have a cook-out at our house."

"Are you?" I said blankly. They often did have them. We could smell the shish kabobs broiling when the wind was right. But cook-outs at the Thaxters had nothing to do with me. Or never had had.

"Yes, and we want you and your mother and . . . well, *you* know, to come."

"Mr. Beard?" I said.

"Anny, don't be mean. You know who."

"Then you must mean Michael Vye. Well, I don't think he'd come."

"And why not? How would you know anyway?"

"He said he was going to hole up completely," I improvised. "He's writing a play, and—"

"I know, I know," Madge interrupted snappishly. "He's a playwright. You don't have to act as if you had a patent on him."

"My goodness, girls," said Maureen, "don't get into such childish wrangles in public." We both looked at her angrily. "Well, excuse *me*," she said, drawing her shoulders together, as if to disassociate herself from us. "I, for one, don't care if your Michael Vye comes or not."

She's ridiculous, I thought, and in my contempt felt less envious. Whatever they had in mind, and what they had in mind was pretty clear, they'd never bring it off with Michael Vye. He was too big for their littleness.

"He isn't a playwright," I said graciously to Madge. "He's a chemist, actually."

"But your mother *said*."

"We didn't know him as well then as we do now."

"He's only been there since yesterday," Maureen snapped. She pulled herself together immediately. "I don't blame him in the least for talking to you freely. Your mother is *such* a sympathetic person. So vital and spry."

"Spry?" I yelled. "She's thirty-five years old. People aren't spry till they're seventy."

"Well, you know what I mean. She's so friendly and full of beans, in spite of her hard life."

37

She sounded patronizing, and I felt protectiveness for my mother rising in me like wrath. I looked witheringly at Maureen and said, "You are handicapped by an imperfect understanding of words. My mother is not spry, *nor* does she have a hard life."

"Well, but she—" Maureen bit her lip and broke off.

"You mean she keeps a boarding house?" I was cold, and faintly nauseated. I suppose I'd known that some people would think of my mother as a boarding house keeper, of me as the landlady's daughter. But I'd known it the way I knew mastodons had once roved the earth. A fact, but one without relevance to things as they were. Now here I was, face to face with a monstrous, irrelevant fact. I leaned forward, till my eyes were only inches from Maureen's, and I said, "You are a spiritual mastodon."

She put her hand on mine, surprising me so that I jumped, and said, "Look, I'm awfully sorry. I didn't mean to insult anybody, certainly not your mother. She's a lovely person."

I was so taken aback and unnerved by her reaction (which I could not help recognizing as a grown-up one) that I cravenly agreed to invite Mother and Mr. Vye to the cook-out, accepted an invitation for myself, and left The Boston Spa in a state of extreme discomposure.

I had no desire to dance around the barbecue pit in the Thaxters' back yard. I didn't think Mother would have, and hoped Michael Vye wouldn't. I felt the way I had one time as a very little girl when, carried away by temporary affection, I'd offered to share my hamster with another little girl. All the way home I'd been filled with bitter, useless self-reproach, wishing I hadn't gone to school that day, or that the other girl had not felt so suddenly friendly toward me, or that I could ever hold my tongue. Vain wishes. She and I alternated the hamster each week till the day he died, and I never really felt close to him again.

I am my own betrayer, I thought as I walked toward the supermarket. I have no one to blame but myself that I seem to tread along the brink of understanding but never really reach it. Twice I realized that I'd been greeted, and turned too late to respond. This sort of thing was defeating, but I would not give up. Opening my eyes as wide as they would go, I looked from face to face, so as to be alert for the next salutation. This one won't catch me napping, I determined, and bumped into Jim Northrup, the baggage master.

"Anny, are you ever going to learn to look where you're going?" he said. "First time I ever saw you, you almost walked under a train."

"Why?"

"How should I know why? Thinking about Peter Rabbit, maybe." He gave a shout of amusement.

Mr. Northrup, who was some sort of cousin to my mother, occasionally had dinner with us, and whenever he did the meals were interrupted by these yells of self-enjoyment and the sound of his big hand coming down on his thigh to emphasize the humor. He was a single man but lived at a railroad man's hotel, not with us. Whenever I encountered him I felt almost tearfully thankful that he was too untidy to pass Mother's rigid requirements for boarders.

Now I resurrected the smile I'd been using in The Boston

Spa and said, "How are you, Cousin Jim? Ridden any good railroads lately?" This was the way I talked with him, on the theory of fighting inanity with inanity.

"Yep. Went to Boston and back the other day." He scratched his head. "Same day that fellow came to your house."

"Yesterday," I pointed out.

"That so? Tempis fidgets, don't it? How do you like him?"

"Like who?"

"That fellow," he said patiently. "One that came to town yesterday."

"He's all right."

"A very nice guy," Cousin Joe said thoughtfully, and I gave up pretending indifference.

"How do you mean?" I asked.

"Oh . . . you take a person like that, educated, young, nothing to do with somebody like me, you know? And when Mick, the conductor, told me he was coming here, I leaned over and said, 'Understand you're heading for my home town,' and he turned round friendly as you please and we got talking and pretty soon he came around and sat with me and we passed the rest of the trip together, gabbing."

"What about?"

He looked blank. "Can't say as I can say. What about? Oh, politics, labor, agriculture. Everything."

Looking at Cousin Jim enviously, I experienced an aspect of love I'd known nothing of before. The sense of deprivation. The knowledge that when I was excluded from it other people had the privilege of his presence. Cousin Jim, his uncle, Mr. Vye, the people at his university, and—my heart seemed actually to lower and grow chill—women. Or girls. Of an age to respond to him freely, without timorousness or apology, without the special pleading that I would have to offer. They wouldn't need to beg him, in words or signs, to see, if he could, what they would one day be, to wait, if he would, only a few short years while they shed this false, betraying cocoon of childishness. In the security of their eighteen or more years they could face and entice him.

While I? How could I have him, entice him?

Images fanned around my mind like moths—blurry, sensuous, mysterious, intolerable. I had enemies. They could not be assailed or confronted. They were impregnable, unknown, but my enemies, and there was too much happening to me all at once.

Standing beside Cousin Jim in the white afternoon sun, I remembered another summer, another man. I was five years old and my father (of whom I thought or remembered little any more) was leaning over me, big-bodied, enormously protective, enormously kind. He was saying, "It's all right, Anny, everything's all right. You've had a little too much excitement but you just take it easy and everything will be fine."

I was lying on the grass and I didn't move or speak. Silently grateful for his bigness blotting out the strong sun, I listened to him tell me that everything was all right.

I had wandered away from the picnic, picking wild flowers for Mother, and, when I'd turned to go back, couldn't find the way. I didn't know where anybody was, or where I was, and I began to run, scattering flowers and shrieking, shrieking. There was a crow shrieking, too, and I thought he was

41

flying over me and might even descend and beat at me with his black wings. Then I fell over a rock and cut my leg, and I was too hurt, too hot, too overwhelmed to run any more. The crow flew away and I lay sobbing, no longer hoping for anything.

Then my father was there. He tore off the sleeve of his shirt to bind my leg, and I was proud to have him make such a rending gesture for me. He picked me up and carried me back across the field, a long way. I remembered, now, how it had been, being in his arms. I remembered how I had believed him when he said that everything was all right. All these years and his death later I longed for my father as if he were newly gone from me. I wanted him to say to me, "It's all right, Anny. You've just had a little too much excitement." I wanted him to blot out the heat of the day, to carry me in his arms.

"Anny, what's the matter?" said Cousin Jim, and I realized that people had been asking me that, one way or another, too often. I was going to have to collect myself before everything I wanted hidden was written across my forehead like a sign blinking on and off.

I managed to smile. "Nothing, Cousin Jim. I have my troubles, like everyone else, you know. But nothing important."

"Troubles?" he snorted. "A little girl like you? Get along."

So I got along. I had marketing to do, and then I was going to go home and ask Mother if I could buy a dress, or even two dresses. "Everything will be all right," I said to myself. "Just take it easy, and everything will be fine."

42

CHAPTER *FOUR*

On Saturday afternoons Mother's friend came. His name was Bertram Wade and he sold automobiles in Kittery, where he lived with his ancient, invalided, demanding, authoritative mother, who, I had decided, was to Mr. Wade as a sponge is to water. I supposed he couldn't help it and held nothing against him, but I sometimes wondered why Mother, who was fond of him (I had never put it to myself more strongly than that), didn't become impatient. When I asked myself impatient for what, I didn't like any possible answer, and finally stopped thinking about it.

At the time of Michael Vye's arrival, Mother and Mr. Wade had known each other for four years, and to my not unfriendly, but certainly unobservant, eye their relationship hadn't altered in that time. They'd met when he sold Mother our second-hand jeep, a useful, ugly vehicle in which Mother looked adorably out of place and knew it. Two weeks after we bought it, he drove over from Kittery to "see if it was working properly," and since then, fair weather or foul, on Saturday shortly after lunch Mr. Wade was with us. He'd never spent a night under our roof, though a few times there'd been storms that even he couldn't face (it interested me how so slender and apparently yielding a person could confront weather that made strong men throw up their hands), and he'd put up at the Farmer's Hotel downtown.

So far as I could see, they were no different with each other now than they'd been that first Saturday, except that after a few months they got to a first-name basis and stalled there.

The summer before, I'd suggested that he spend his vacation with us. "He could use the attic room," I'd pointed out, feeling rather maternal toward them both, thinking what fun it would be for them to have some real time together. I foresaw no risk in my offer. When Mother hesitated, I added, "With all of us in this house, you know, people would never talk."

"Well, I should think not," Mother said. "Bert and I have never given people the slightest reason to talk." If she sounded wistful, I didn't notice it. "But it's impossible, Anny. His mother wouldn't tolerate it."

"What is he, a man or a mouse?" I said, and waited for Mother to snap at me. She didn't. She rubbed her forehead with the back of her hand and said, "He's a man who cannot bear to cause hurt."

I said cautiously, "Is his mother the only one who's being hurt?"

"You oil what squeaks the loudest," Mother said in a dry

tone, quite unlike her. "She swoons and screams and foresees her own death if he gets out a suitcase. He can't stand that, so he gives in."

"Well," I said, meaning to comfort, "maybe she will die."

"Anny, don't *talk* that way," Mother said sharply, and then, with what I considered real inconsistence, added, "Anyway, her spleen should keep her going into perpetuity."

But usually she didn't talk to me this way, and sometimes I forgot him completely, until Mother, as if she'd been thinking of him all along, would say, "Bert tells me it's going to be an early fall this year," or, "Let's have lamb Saturday evening, Lenore. Bert's so fond of it," and I'd remember that this man was now part of our lives.

Lenore accepted and liked him, but that was because, like Mother, he seemed attentive to her endless talk. Almost the first day he came she cornered him and was grinding on about "my daughter in Annapolis Maryland got two cute little kids boy and a girl cutest little things you've ever seen and how they love Grandma can't wait for her that's me to get down there and tell them stories and maybe give them a dollar if they act real nice I have their pictures right here see what'd I tell you that's Kenny and that there is Sue yup Annapolis Maryland. . . ."

Half an hour after Lenore arrived I was usually swarming up the walls in an effort to escape, but Mother and Mr. Wade just listened and smiled as she went on and on, never punctuating, pausing fractionally to gasp for breath, producing only a loose progression of purely personal ideas. They listened and she doted on them.

The Saturday after Michael Vye came I was sitting on the

porch, wearing my new dress, practicing kindness and curiosity on Mr. Beard (I had thought of starting on Lenore,
but my courage seeped at her first syllable) when Mr. Wade
turned into the driveway, and got out, carrying a package.
He always brought some offering on his visits. A bright piece
of ovenware, a new kind of coffeemaker, a carving set. Practical, impersonal things. Once in a while I'd thought of sug-
gesting to him that he buy Mother a bottle of perfume, or a
scarf, something just for her. But I never did.

I got up, straightening my skirt, thinking this a good opportunity to take leave of Mr. Beard.

"Hi, Mr. Wade," I called. "Mother's in the kitchen.
What've you got there?"

"Oh, a nothing, Anny. Like I got it in a fire sale."

Mr. Wade was very nice about trying to speak what he
thought was my language. The fact that he didn't know what
it was made him no less nice, but sometimes I was embar-
rassed for him. After a dutiful smile, I turned back to Mr.
Beard. He was looking mutely, resignedly disappointed, and
I was suddenly ashamed. Here I'd been drawing him out for
purposes of my own, and, truth to tell, scarcely listening to
what he told me, because he really was such a prosy old man,
and then I'd leaped to my feet with an obvious wish and will
to be gone at the first opportunity. He was unprotesting. If I
hadn't turned I wouldn't have known that he was also
saddened and tired by my desertion, or all desertions.

I thought, but this must happen to him over and over.
Somebody gives him a moment's attention, and he hurries
and tries to tell everything quickly before they go. He'd been
explaining to me about what winters were like in New Eng-

46

land when he was a boy. At least, I thought he'd been. Maybe he'd gotten on to something else. So many men did talk about New England winters when they'd been young. My father had done it. Cousin Jim still did. And Mr. Wade, and the minister, and the manager of the supermarket. It was not a thing that women ever talked about, but men loved to.

For the first time I really looked at Mr. Beard. Not through or around, but at him. A skinny, knobbly old man wearing clean bedraggled khakis and a faded blue shirt open at his bony throat. He had big feet and a bald bumpy skull, and the hands with which he now tried unconcernedly to fill his pipe trembled a little. Pity is not a youthful emotion. I doubt I'd ever felt it till that moment, but looking at Mr. Beard then I wanted to station myself like a maiden warrior between him and his fate, which was to be old and ignored.

"Well," I said, settling beside him as if Mr. Wade's arrival had been an interruption. "*Well!*"

I waited for him to resume, in his quick, clackety voice, whatever it was he'd been saying. But he sat in silence, attending to the pipe, his eyes fixed on the bowl as if there were messages in there.

"I remember my father," I went on, "telling me about the blizzards of his boyhood. Actually, Mr. Beard, I don't remember *too* much about my father, you know. He died when I was very little."

I expected that to draw him out, and it did.

"I remember him," he began slowly. "Better than you do, I suppose. His father and I were stationed at Bragg together in the war."

"Which war was that?" I asked, really having no idea.

47

"First World War," Mr. Beard said. He lit a match, put the pipe to his mouth, began to draw on it, puffing rapidly, sending out clouds of sweet smoke. In a little while he said, "Numbering's a good way to keep track of things, but I guess they won't have to use up many numbers on these wars."

He often talked this way. He expected another war. He said an irresponsible species like the human one wouldn't be able to have world destruction within its power and not take a chance on seeing what it would be like. I got the feeling that he would have liked to wash his hands of people altogether, but couldn't because he was dependent on them to listen to his views. I now think that he was always looking for someone to deny his prophecies, to tell him that man, however flawed, was not, in the final analysis, self-destructive. Since he had no relatives, nor long to live himself, Mr. Beard was more tenderly solicitous of the human race than his words told, or we realized.

So far as I was concerned, he might have been talking about Indian raids. He simply didn't reach me. Mother always said, "Oh, please, Mr. Beard, don't. You frighten me," and Mrs. Halley would scowl and tell him to keep his horrible notions to himself.

Now, not to deflect him, but because he had stopped talking again, I said, "Tell me about my father, Mr. Beard. I just remember that he was big. A big man, and very kind. I mean, I remember a few separate incidents, like one time when I got lost at a picnic and he found me, and another time when he took me on an overnight trip to Bangor. But practically nothing."

"He was like his own father," Mr. Beard said. "Kind, as you say. And improvident. You know what that means?"

I nodded, realizing that I was as enigmatic to Mr. Beard as he was to me. All we knew about each other was that he was old and I was young. Still, there we were, attempting to establish communication, he because of his need to have contact with someone, and I because my schoolgirl arrogance had led me to a new emotion.

"Improvident people," he said, "are very often kind. And surprisingly often they are big, physically. I suppose it's that little people, like me, fight to keep what they've gotten, in case there isn't any more, but big people—"

I saw that we weren't going to talk much about my father. Mr. Beard, in the few years I knew him, never did talk about individuals, except to use some reference to one as a pathway to his own sort of generality. I listened to his theories about generosity and bulk, glad that he was talking, and thinking to myself that he was one person physically little who hadn't managed to keep much of what he'd gotten. Once he'd owned a drugstore. Now he lived on Social Security, in a boarding house, grateful for a child's attention.

So for the first time in my life I knew pity. At first it was for Mr. Beard himself. Then, as he spoke, for all lonely old men. Before he died, five years later, Mr. Beard had taught me some compassion and ruth—that was his own odd and lovely word—for Man himself. Poor Man, trying to understand what it is he really wants and can give.

I'd elected to be kind and curious in order to enchant Michael Vye, so it was ironical that when Michael himself came whistling out of the house I could scarcely take a moment to greet him. Whatever it was Mr. Beard was trying to tell me (and I could understand less than half of it) my attention was so acutely important that to turn, as I wished, to that face of all faces and lose myself in contemplation of it would be a more arrant desertion than following Mr. Wade could possibly have been.

Trying to tamp my agitation down, I half-waved at Michael, keeping my eyes on Mr. Beard, nervously sure that I looked less like somebody showing kindly curiosity than like a person trying not to scratch an itch. I shifted around and said, "Oh, do go on," to Mr. Beard, who as a matter of fact *was* going on, and then wondered if in being attentive to the older man I wasn't being rude to the younger, so turned slightly, then whipped my head back again, figuring I might as well go all the way in one direction rather than halfway in none.

Mercifully, Mr. Beard decided at that moment to recognize Michael Vye. "Hello, there," he said, in a sort of expansive way, as if he were holding court. "Wish to join us?"

Michael hesitated, then shook his head. "Thanks, anyway, but I've been sitting up there working all morning. I want to stretch my legs." He looked at me inquiringly. "Want to take a walk? Or are you—" He stopped.

Mr. Beard's cane, propped against the porch railing, obviously precluded him from the invitation—Michael Vye was a fast walker—and Michael apparently decided his invitation was improper. He said, "I may want to walk too long for you, anyway, Anny. See you both," and went down the steps, along the path, out the gate, where he turned to the left, toward the country, and set off.

I could not, for pain or pity's sake, prevent myself from staring until he was lost behind the high privet backing the Thaxters' fence.

"For mankind to go gadding around in space," Mr. Beard was saying, "is the most irrational kind of stupidity. It's like giving a driver's license to a ten-year-old child. Let us enlighten ourselves as to our course on earth before we attempt to chart and navigate the outer world. What we need in this time is teachers, not astronauts."

I pulled my sight and thoughts from the empty, sun-dappled road and tried to fix them on this man who was being a teacher to me, though not in the way he intended.

Thousands of words later, with a sated sigh, he waved me off, saying he'd just lean back now and take a little snooze. Like many another tyro to unselfishness, I experienced a flash of discontent, feeling that my attention had not been sufficiently appreciated. Then I studied the pale, lined face, closed lids protecting the faded eyes, and thought I saw an expression there that was new—a faint smile at his mouth, an attitude of sturdy comfort in his pose that stayed within him even as I watched and he fell asleep.

I checked to see that his cane was within reach and walked slowly into the house, closing the screen door behind me with care. Forgetful of Michael Vye and even of myself, I wandered as if listening still. Not to words. To a prelude, perhaps. An overture with some of the notes missing, but more included than had been there just that morning.

Attentive to this distant orchestra, I was almost in the kitchen when Mother's voice, plaintively unfamiliar, spoke from behind the swinging door.

"Bert, *what* do you expect me to do, or say to you? Of course I love you. More than anything else in the world. But I'm not *made* of understanding. How do you think I feel, left alone all week, visited on a schedule your mother permits? What do you think I say to my friends? Do you think they never ask where I'm going, never make remarks about wedding bells and cakes with little candy brides and grooms on top? I *want* a cake with a little candy bride and groom. I want to be able to *be* with you, openly, always. I'm tired of being treated like a shameful secret."

"Nan, Nan, don't," moaned Mr. Wade. "Please don't."

I did not consider that I was listening to something I had no right to hear, nor did I consider moving tactfully and silently away. I had a right to hear, and stood my ground in misery.

"If I'm a pastime," Mother was saying, "then tell me so. Let me at least know what my role is. Then maybe I'll know better how to act. If I'm to be a weekend woman forever, then *tell* me—"

"Nan!" he cried out in shocked, shocking tone. "Nan!" He did not seem to be able to say anything but "Nan!" like that, over and over.

I told myself I wouldn't have known my mother. Yet I suppose this hurt and bitter woman was someone I recognized. She was the woman who'd come weeping forward when my father died. The woman who had held me too close

52

and released me too quickly, again and again, at that time of loss I scarcely comprehended. Here was that long-quiescent woman come forth again, and I trembled at her resurgence.

She was crying, and then abruptly she stopped. Her voice when she spoke again was tender, as it was to me when I was sick. More tender.

"Bert," she said, "Bert, dearest. Don't let me talk to you this way. Don't let me do this. You *mustn't* let anybody do this to you."

"But you have every right to," he said. "Every right. And what you say is true."

"No. No right at all. And the only truth is that we love each other. As long as we know that, everything else will take care of itself. Let's just remember that."

"Remember it?" he said hoarsely. "It's what I have. All I have."

If he kisses her, I thought, I won't be able to bear it. Turning, I ran down the hall and out the screen door. It banged behind me, waking Mr. Beard.

"Anny!" he called, almost peremptorily. And then, "Anny," as if he were pleading. But I fled down the road, nearly a half-mile, into the arms of Michael Vye.

It's Fate, I told myself, leaning against him. He is my fate. Nothing else is important, no one else matters. Mother will do what she must, but I belong to Michael Vye.

He stood me away, hands on my shoulders, and said, "Hey, hey, what's this?" like somebody's uncle, or a man setting a strange child on its feet.

"I'm running away," I gasped.

"From what?"

"From home," I said wildly, not expecting to be believed, but wanting to alarm somebody.

"Where's your luggage?"

"Don't *laugh* at me!" I flared.

He grimaced. "I'm not laughing at you. I'm trying to understand what's going on. You can't be running away, so what are you doing?"

Panting, shaking with nerves and exertion, I glared up into his eyes, and he shook me slightly, in a stern, corrective manner. I tried to lean against him again, but he wouldn't permit it.

"Over here," he said, leading me off the road, up a little rise, down in the hollow at the other side. "Now," he said, "sit down, and tell me what it's about."

I couldn't tell him anything. I looked into his gray eyes, and found nothing to say that would not make me sound like a spying, jealous child.

Which, I told myself coldly, I am. Only with reason. I had a feeling the reasons would have validity for no one but myself. Anyone could tell that Michael Vye was a man of understanding, but it would require more than understanding to understand me. It would take, I thought with no sense of undue self-importance, Omnipotence.

"I don't have anything to say," I told him.

He accepted that. "Well, catch your breath for a minute, and we'll go home."

"How funny of you. Do you really think of our place as home?"

"While I'm here I do, yes."

"It actually feels homelike to you?"

"Well, yes, it does. You sound as if you disapproved."

"Oh, no. No, I don't. I love you to feel that way. It's . . . hard to understand, that's all. A boarding house in a small town. Mr. Beard and Mrs. Halley for dining companions . . ."

"Your mother is there. And you," he added.

"Still—I'm glad you do. How is the play coming?"

"Resisting every step of the way. In my lucid moments I wonder what backward devil has possession of me, persuading me that I can be a man of letters."

"How long have you been working on it?"

"Months, off and on. This summer is to kill or cure, you know. I said to myself, I'll get away somewhere and give this Muse the benefit of every doubt, and then if she doesn't come through, I wash my hands of her."

"I don't see why," I said sincerely. "She might be the sort of Muse who needs a lifetime of off-and-on attention, not just a summer's worth. Wouldn't it be awful if you quit and it was really in your future somewhere to write a great play?"

"Little fear," he said, smiling. "How nice you are."

"No, but I really mean it," I said, too shy to accept his words easily. "Maybe you're Shakespeare," I added, and knew at once I'd gone too far, as I often did when excited or very much moved.

Oh, it's all too much, I said to myself tiredly. Everything's too much. I was suddenly desperately sleepy. My lids felt thick and heavy, my knees still trembled a little, and I wanted to stop thinking, feeling, being. The sun seemed to be blazing now, drawing thick scents out of the parched meadow grass, making trees in the distance waver. A butterfly fanned languidly by, moving its wings slowly, as if with effort. I watched it stupidly, hearing Michael Vye's voice beside me, and then I could follow neither the butterfly's progress nor the man's words . . .

I came to with someone shaking my shoulder gently. I thought it was Mother and didn't want her near me. "Stop it, stop it!" I cried out, and opened my eyes to Michael's face.

"I'm sorry," he said, sounding concerned. "I just didn't think you should go to sleep here."

Thickly, dazedly, I looked around and blinked. "Excuse me. I don't know what I was thinking of. Did I go to sleep for long?"

"Not at all. You were just dozing off. Why don't you go home and take a nap, Anny? Let's go back and I'll tell your mother—"

"No! I mean, please . . . let me . . . that is, Mother is busy. Mr. Wade's here for his Saturday afternoon and I don't want to disturb them. I'm quite able to take care of myself, you know."

"Yes, of course you are," he said too readily, as one does to a child.

I wanted to say, "Will you please look at me? Will you use your eyes and your heart and recognize that I am very nearly a woman, I am just at the very edge of being one, and if you would see that and wait a little while, only a little while, I would be ready for you. In three years, in two even, I would not be too young for you, for your desire, for your love . . ."

But he was up, dusting off the seat of his trousers, impatient to be moving, and unassisted I got to my feet with everything unsaid.

There was no sign of Mr. Beard when we turned in at the gate, and I was grateful for that. Michael left me, saying he should probably go up and see if that Muse was hanging around with a few ideas.

"Oh, she's probably there, reading your mail, with her feet on the desk," I said half-heartedly.

He laughed and went up the stairs quickly. I watched till he reached the landing, but he didn't turn around. Then, with trepidation, I went toward the kitchen, coughing and making as noisy an arrival as possible. Mother was at the table, shelling peas, her head bent.

"Where's Mr. Wade?" I said.

She looked up. She was terribly pale, her cheeks and lips colorless. Even her hair seemed to have lost its brightness. "Gone," she said. The brightness, the color, had left her voice, too.

"Gone?" I repeated. "Gone where?"

"Home."

"Why? He was here just an hour ago," I said, deliberately cruel. Had she not told me, too, many times, that she loved me more than anything in the world? Why should I not be cruel? "What was in the package?"

Mother closed her eyes briefly, opened them, gestured toward the sideboard. "That—" She stopped, took a breath, started again, "that—" On the third try she managed to say, "That roll basket. It's . . . pretty, isn't it?"

At once I was shaken with remorse. No matter what she said to both Mr. Wade and me (and I thought that perhaps in different ways a woman could love both a man and a child more than anything in the world) she was my mother, and she was suffering. From whatever it was he did or did not do, and from my childishness, my baiting. She was very brave. I hadn't known that before, and I looked at her with respect, if not with the old adoration.

"Could I take a nap before I do my chores?" I asked after a minute. "I'm awfully tired."

She tucked back a fallen lock of hair and nodded. "You're getting to be like an old woman, Anny. Always having to lie down. If you're sick, I wish you'd tell me. We could get you to the doctor—"

"I'm not sick," I interrupted. "Just . . . Oh, just a little weary of things. And I don't really want a nap, I want to be alone."

"That's reasonable," she said.

It occurred to me that I should offer to let her have the hour's respite one of us was going to have. I didn't want to, but managed with an effort to say, "Listen, why don't you go to your room, instead? I'll take care of things down here."

She looked tempted, then shook her head. "It's better if . . . I mean, I'd just as soon keep busy this afternoon, Anny. Thank you for being so thoughtful."

I avoided her eyes, having never in my life been less thoughtful for her. Her pain, her thwarted lovingness, her loneliness, her very bravery were just threats to me. I realized that all along today, and recently, I'd been resenting Mother's having problems of her own at a time when mine were so demanding and absorbing. Hasn't she had enough? I thought, angry again. Isn't it my turn, my time now?

Unable to bear or consider competition with my own mother—there seemed to be something almost indecent in it—I ran out of the room and up to my retreat, the wide window seat beside the sycamore. Tabu, my innocent companion, leaped up and settled down, purring, happy to be with me, not inquiring further. How I was feeling affected her not at all; she just wanted me to be there. She kneaded her claws on my thigh, her eyes closed. Her very fur seemed to smooth itself peacefully because I was with her. She had nothing to think of; I had too much. Putting my hand on her round head, two fingers pressing gently in the hollows at the inside edges of her ears, I tried to be like her—mindless, at peace.

We sat there—one of us purring, the other saying to herself, "Take it easy, and everything will be all right. Take it easy, and—"

Over and over.

CHAPTER *FIVE*

"Ever since that man came here," Mrs. Halley grumbled, "things have been different, and I don't like it."

"I don't know what you mean," I said. "Oh, look, Mrs. Halley, if you put that jack of spades on the ten—"

"That's what he reminds me of," she interrupted. "He looks like the jack of spades. A troublemaker."

I was arrested by this notion. Not that I'd ever thought of the jack of spades as especially troublesome (Mrs. Halley related to her cards in a highly personal way), but I liked romantic notions of Michael Vye. Sydney Carton, the jack of spades . . . no ordinary man put ideas like that in the beholder's head.

"Ever since he came," Mrs. Halley persisted. "Even your mother's cooking has fallen off, if you ask me."

"I didn't," I said coldly. "And it hasn't."

"Oh, well," she mumbled. I took it to be an apology, or

the closest to one that she could come, and we went on with the game in silence for a while.

But, of course, everything was changed, and it had not required Mrs. Halley to point it out. I didn't know about the food, because I was eating next to nothing, but Mother herself was strangely altered. If I had not been solely occupied with trying to find some equilibrium in my own rocking, pitching world, I would have worried about her.

I saw this wan, smudgy-eyed stranger going about the house in pursuit of her landlady's duties, speaking little, starting at small sounds, anxiously eying and then looking away from the telephone, and only now and then did I remember the beloved being who'd once made life seem like a piece of lucky magic. For a while I'd resented her torment, now I was indifferent to it. *Sauve qui peut*, I'd say to myself in my own restless wanderings, my search for a place to be . . .

Everything rejected me. Books, fancy, the hiding spot at the end of the garden. There was no place to be, nowhere to go. I ended up playing solitaire with Mrs. Halley.

Everything was changing, sadly and far too quickly. But it is not, I said to myself, shaking one of Mrs. Halley's sticky old cards loose from my fingers, it is not the fault of Michael Vye. He has nothing even to do with Mother's misery, and is the utterly unwitting author of mine. He just came to write his play in peace and eat at my mother's highly recommended board. How can this silly sheep blame him for anything?

"You liked him very much at the beginning," I said suddenly.

"He misled me. I thought him sympathetic, but I couldn't have been wronger. He's really pretty cold-hearted. And he didn't fool me for long, let me tell you."

He got tired of listening to her slander that poor daughter-in-law, I decided. Michael Vye was not a man to suffer fools—especially spiteful fools—gladly. Neither was he one to listen indefinitely to old men predicting the world's end. So the happy welcome of that first evening had soon cooled off, leaving Mrs. Halley more spiteful than ever, Mr. Beard icily silent whenever Michael was present. But I could see why Mrs. Halley wanted to put the onus on the newcomer since, innocent though he was, everything *had* started to fall apart shortly after his arrival.

It was late afternoon, and hot. We were in the living room, with blinds drawn against the sun, the atmosphere dusky and oppressive. There was hardly any sound or movement in the rest of the house. Lenore was out. Mr. Beard was napping. We could never hear Michael Vye's typewriter from down here. I could hear the clock in the hall, the creakings that were always with us, the thrum of the washing machine that Mother had put on before she went downtown. It was the first time she'd been out in a week, and she'd made sure before leaving that I was going to be around. For the telephone, I told myself, thinking what a pathetic reversal of roles this was. Shouldn't the daughter be the one circling the phone like a moth around a lamp? Surely it wasn't the mother's place?

But Mother was acting less and less maternal, more and more like a person, and I wondered, turning my fury abruptly to Mr. Wade, where it was all going to end. What had he in mind, anyway, with his rushing off and his long silence, after those words he'd spoken to her in the kitchen? He'd said her love was what he had, all he had. Was it his decision then to do without her, in spite of having nothing to take her place? Or, for that matter, *did* he have someone besides his enveloping mother? How could you tell what people's words meant? Or what their silence meant?

"When I remember," Mrs. Halley said, "how sweet and chirpy your mother always was, with a good word for everyone, and that gorgeous smile, well, I tell you I could just cry, that's all." She peered at me closely, to see how I was taking this. "If you and your mother don't watch out, this place will lose its reputation." She thought that over, and added quickly, "I don't mean that the way it sounds, and of course your mother *never* gives rise to talk, no matter how—how spirited she is. Was. I mean, its reputation as a place that's comfy and all, the sort of boarding house everybody wants to get into." She stopped again, this time definitely waiting for a response from me.

I considered a moment, and then said, "I don't care how you mean it."

Down went the cards, up went her chin, out came the tirade I'd known perfectly well would be provoked by those words. I listened to the malicious, threatening flow, my head to one side, thinking how gratifying it was to anger an adult. Particularly when I felt so unconcerned. I observed the way rage empurpled her face, noted the manner in which it tangled her words, with the detached interest I'd have accorded a squawking chicken, and though she was not a subtle woman, my attitude got through to her.

"Very well," she said, gathering her deck of cards and rising to her feet, "very *well!*"

It was simple enough to read menace into that, and I

began to feel uncomfortable. Doubtless she'd complain to my mother, but that was not my real worry. In her old mood, Mother would have been on my side. In her new one, she probably wouldn't be on anybody's. I was worried for fear Mrs. Halley would leave us. Not too desperate an eventuality, except that she could be so horribly unpleasant. I could just hear her. "The daughter's rude and badly brought up, and the mother moons around about men." I shivered with disgust, realizing I'd have to try conciliation.

"Mrs. Halley," I said, and had to swallow a bitter taste before I could continue, "Mrs. Halley . . . excuse me. I shouldn't have said that."

"People who think they can say anything they please!" she snapped at me. "They make me sick."

You should know about that, I thought, getting to my feet, not wanting to be beneath her eye level. "Excuse me," I said again. She looked at me avidly, waiting for more of the same, but I was spent.

It occurred to me that I could offer to run an errand for her, which she would be free to interpret as groveling. It would get me out of her society. Mrs. Halley was careful not to let herself be imposed upon (she called it maintaining her self-respect, and it was this self-respect that her daughter-in-law had violated, probably by refusing to let her own be tampered with) but she was willing enough to impose. What she called this, I don't know. Self-assertion, maybe.

In any case, she was constantly asking me to do large or little services for her that she was too indolent to take care of herself. Until recently I hadn't minded. My time was not taken up, as was that of other girls I knew, with dates and boys and the worrying over them. I could always take a book along and read it on the bus as I went downtown for her face cream, or her light novels from the library, or whatever. It gave me a chance to get away from the house, where there'd just be something else for me to do. I liked wandering downtown by myself, and I loved poking around the library, finding my own books as well as Mrs. Halley's.

Now all that was altered. I wanted to be home, in the radius of Michael Vye, who, even if he stayed pretty much hidden in his room most of the day, was an all-absorbing presence. There was always the chance that he'd wander downstairs, looking for a snack. Two or three times he'd asked me, in his offhand way, to accompany him on one of those walks he took, which were too long and fast for me, but which I cherished above comfort or ease. We didn't talk much those times, but when he did speak he seemed to me to possess wisdom that was ageless and splendid. Neither of us had ever referred to that day when I ran trembling into his arms, and I'd returned to my childlike camouflage, which made us feel safe with each other, and freed me to ask questions of him that an actual adult never would have dared.

So it was only extremity that drove me to say, "Do you want any new books, Mrs. Halley? I could go down to the library and get you some."

She wavered between wanting to avail herself of an unexpected offer (she'd gotten her own books the last two times) and wanting to scare me some more. She had a true bully's instinct for when the other person was alarmed.

Laziness won out. "I *would* like to have a new book or so," she admitted. "Actually I got one I'd already read—these titles are so confusing—and now I have only a few pages left of the other one. If you just run upstairs, they're on the table beside my bed." She gave me a saccharine smile as I started off. "Now don't you worry about anything, Anny. You were a little rude just now, but you and I know it's just growing pains, don't we? So we won't say anything about it to anyone."

She had decided I was penitent, and was forgiving me. With an effort I smiled back but could not bring myself to say anything except, "I'll get the books, then, and be on my way."

On the bus I suddenly remembered Mother and the phone call she was hoping to get. For a moment I considered getting off at the next stop and going back, positive that now of all times would be the one selected by Fate and Mr. Wade for the call to be made. If he was anything like me—finding omens everywhere—he would probably consider Mrs. Halley's answering voice a sign of the illest sort. It might even cause him to hang up and never call again. I started to rise, then leaned back again.

What if he did call, hoping for Mother's eager, forgiving voice, and getting instead Mrs. Halley's snoopy, acidulous one? What if he should decide that the omens were unpropitious? If it put him off forever, what of that? After a while, surely Mother would piece together her fragmented self and be as good as new, as sweet as before? She couldn't behave like an emotionally displaced person forever. She got over my father's death, I told myself, and that was really important. She can get over the defections of gentle, spineless Mr. Wade.

By the time I reached the library I was thinking of him mournfully, remembering how nice he'd been, in how many different ways. I had put him out of Mother's life and mine, consigned him to nothingness, with a little ritual of sadness because he'd really been a very nice man.

I closed the library door behind me and stood for a moment, inhaling its essence. It was always the same when I came here, as if I'd come not to a place but to a moment in time, one that never had changed and never would. The mixture of odors—wax and paste, leather and dust—was easy and familiar. The sun came through the Venetian blinds and fell across the stacks and the floors in combs of light in a way that was never altered. Miss Fillmore's desk and its arrangement were immutable—the stamping machine, the pencils, the paper clips, the pottery bowl of cosmos (or zinnias, or pine sprigs). And Miss Fillmore, imperishable priestess of the temple, there since I could remember, and there, if I thought of it, forevermore. My home, my mother, my thoughts, my life could alter out of all recognition, but the moment I stepped into this place I knew where I was.

Maybe, I thought wryly, I should just take a blanket and move down here. I can't read any more, but at least I could rely on the surroundings not to crouch and leap and flicker like shadows before a fire. And I would not be driven mad by "seems," a word with an inky, endless wingspread. Mother seemed, life seemed, Michael seemed, I seemed, but where was footing in all this seeming? *"Nay, madam, I know not 'seems,'"* I said to myself. Here, at least, it concerned me not. Books were books, Miss Fillmore was Miss Fillmore, and the sun on the stacks concealed nothing at all. It only revealed.

"Anny," said Miss Fillmore in her low, restrained voice. "How nice to see you."

I dropped Mrs. Halley's lending-library novels on the desk. "Hi, Miss Fillmore. Mrs. Halley says she'd already read one of these, so she shouldn't have to pay for it." Miss Fillmore sniffed a little but didn't argue. "I have to get her two more."

"None for yourself?" Miss Fillmore said curiously. "Have you inherited a private collection? You haven't taken out a book in over a month."

I hesitated, feeling somewhat abashed, as if I'd let her down, and considered offering an eye affliction as excuse. But lying, even simple lying, never came easily to me, and I was tired of evasion. If this was the one place I was sure of, then surely it was the one place in which to be straightforward. Disguises with Michael, hypocrisy with Mrs. Halley, guile with Mr. Beard, a sort of skittish insincerity with my mother—that seemed to be my portion of late. Only here I would not have it.

"I haven't been reading at all," I said, and waited to ease her dismay, though I was unsure how. Perhaps a promise of better things to come—

I realized that she'd scarcely been touched by dismay. Now I felt let down. Didn't she care that I, one of the town's most promising, dedicated readers, had apparently abjured everything she and the library represented? Shouldn't the priestess of the stacks put up more of a fight when a self-avowed apostate was right within her grasp?

"I haven't been sick, either," I said. "I just can't seem to care about books any more. They don't *mean* anything." How could I put it so that she'd realize the extent of my heresy, my loss? *See here, Miss Fillmore,* I wanted to shout in the quiet room, *do you understand what I'm telling you?*

All the same, she did not. She fiddled with some cards, smiled at me pleasantly, and said it wasn't surprising that in the heat of the summer I'd found something other to do than read. As if it were pretty unimportant. As if, in fact, it didn't matter at all. She got a couple of books out from some hiding place and said these were brand new, so Mrs. Halley wouldn't be able to say she'd read either of them. I took them in silence and left, feeling that the last haven had closed its doors to me.

Within half a block a horn tooted and I turned to see Mother in the jeep. Catching her image unexpectedly that way, I saw I hadn't been exaggerating the alteration in her. She looked tense and thin, and though she smiled in the old way, it hadn't the old untrammeled sparkle. She was forcing herself to smile in welcome when she would rather have been alone, and I forced myself to the side of the jeep, wishing we hadn't chanced to meet.

She asked what I'd been doing, and I explained that Mrs. Halley had proved too difficult to stay with, so I'd offered to get the books for her just to get away.

"That's nice," said Mother, naturally assuming I'd had a happy time. She often referred to the library as "Anny's home away from home."

I wanted to say, "Look, it isn't that way at all. I didn't have a happy time there, and I may never go back again. There isn't any place left that I belong, except the window seat in my room. Am I to spend the rest of my life on a window seat?"

Probably I wouldn't have said it. I was melodramatic within the walls of my mind but did not much care for being so out loud. In any case, Mother was not awaiting outcries of that nature from me. She jiggled the shift in neutral, sighed, and said, "Anyone call?"

I shook my head. "Nope. I mean, not while I was there. I'm sorry, Mother. For leaving, I mean."

"Oh . . . don't worry about that, Anny. I shouldn't have asked you to stay."

"It was perfectly fine. I mean, I didn't mind in the least."

It wasn't an easy conversation to sustain, and Mother decided not to try. She put her hand out and patted my arm briefly, then smiled again, this time with something of the old humor, and said, "Let's play hooky for a while."

It was as if months, or even years, had dropped away, and I remembered how in the past she would astonish me by saying, "Let's play hooky" at just the moment when I could march no farther on the indicated road.

That time I'd come home when I was—how old? Oh, eight or nine—with a note in my pocket from the principal saying I was insubordinate, impertinent, rude, and unacceptable to my peer group. I trudged home in the empty afternoon, sick-hearted, fluttering with alarm, certain I'd be dismissed and never get beyond long division. It didn't occur to me not to go straight to Mother, but I was desperate with shame and apprehension.

Mother read the note, her lower lip thrust out thoughtfully. She looked up at me. "What happened?"

"I kicked a girl. She told the teacher I read her paper. She said I cheated."

"What nonsense."

Warmth stole through my limbs, and I could feel myself getting ready to cry. Then I glanced over at Mother, who was dropping the note in a trash basket. She dusted her hands a little.

"Nothing to do about this today," she said. "I tell you what. Let's go to a movie."

There'd been times—infrequent but intense—when the boarding-house trade had covered me like a cloud and I'd loathed everything—the linen, the fresh garden vegetables, the dinner gong, the furniture wax, and the boarders, the boarders, the boarders.

I'd think to myself, "Not one more demand, not one more complaint, not one more snoopy personal question will I tolerate," and there would be Mother saying, "Anny, let's play hooky." So we'd get Lenore to cope with dinner, and Mother and I would go off. To a movie if the weather were poor. On a picnic. All the way to Boston once, where we stayed overnight in a hotel and went to a symphony concert.

I looked at her now, the old love returning, jumped in the jeep, and said, "I'd adore it. Where to?"

"Well . . . we can't stay out long this time. Lenore will be expecting us. But maybe we could just drive by The House for a while, all right?"

"Okay," I said.

It didn't matter much where we went, it just felt so good to be with her, running away for a little while from the others. We didn't speak as we drove, and at first I took it to be a companionable silence. But little by little I was forced to see that Mother had already relapsed into brooding. She could come out of it for a minute, but not, it seemed, for longer, and this time she was playing hooky on her own account. Apparently it didn't work for her. I wanted to say something bracing, but all I could think of were sort of "do you remember" things, and I wasn't sure those would help.

Nevertheless, "Do you remember," I said, as we drove out the other end of town and along the road toward The House we coveted and economized for and dreamed of (though we hadn't, I realized, spoken much about it lately). "Do you remember that time I was accused of cheating in class and I kicked the girl and got sent home with a note?"

"Of course I remember." But she kept her eyes on the road, and made a great business of avoiding a rock that wasn't really in the way.

"We went to a movie," I persisted in a thin voice. "It was lovely of you."

"That silly sheep," she said suddenly. It was an expression I'd picked up from her and enjoyed using. It was easy to guess her reference to the principal who'd written the note.

"What did you ever say to him?" I asked. "How did I get back in school? What did he say to you?"

"Oh"—she waved an imperious hand—"*he* told *me* that your personality constellation was disturbed."

"For Pete's sake."

"And *I* told *him* that your accuser was mistaken, and probably a downright liar. I suppose I could have been more dignified, but I was awfully angry."

"I know you were," I said comfortably, forgetting again all the years that lay between. More than anything in the world, more even, at that moment, than Michael Vye's love, I wanted to say to her, "You have made me very happy, always, and I love you."

I simply could not do it.

The trials of growth are heavy. The torpor, the dizziness, the tears. The loneliness and the need to be alone. The feeling that you no longer fit your body, that you may not quite rely on your mind. The sense of danger that cannot be averted, of alienation from all that once was certain and stable. Not all of them always present, but all ready to surge forth in a tide like lava any time, any place.

Sitting beside my mother, unable to say what I deeply felt, it was as if not inches but eons, ages, light-years lay between us. I remembered, little more than a month ago, throwing my arms around her for some reason—or none— and saying, "Mother, I *adore* you." Now here I sat, lonely after our moment's closeness, our second of remembering, farther away from her than ever.

You don't only grow up, I thought, you grow away. I felt very original, and stabbed to the heart.

Mother braked the jeep suddenly and cried out, "I tell you it is *more than I can bear!*"

I felt a shudder of alarm, wondering if she'd lost her mind, and then, looking up, echoed her words in my mind.

In front of The House was a sign on the lawn, newly mown where so long it had been a creeping wilderness, that read, Sold, by Finnerty Co."

We sat, stunned, stricken, completely believing.

"Well," Mother said at length, "there's no need to save any more. Maybe we can paint the house now. God knows it needs it."

"But maybe . . . some other place?" I said tentatively.

Mother leaned her elbows on the steering wheel, resting her forehead in her hands. "I don't know," she said in a muffled voice. "I suppose I always thought it was this or nothing."

"I know." My eyes wandered dully over the house. The windows were washed, and the driveway was being repaired. "They're putting radiant heating in the driveway," I said. "I guess the people who bought it are rich."

"Sure they're rich," Mother said bitterly, lifting her head. "He works in Boston and commutes to the office by helicopter. The swimming pool is already on order, and they have a couple of sub-deb daughters . . . named Heidi and Kim. Also a standard poodle and two Siamese cats."

"And a son with one of those biblical names—Matthew or Seth."

"How quickly you catch on," Mother said. She turned to me, shrugged, lifted one eyebrow, and laughed once again. I caught a flash of the old ardor, and I said to myself, if this is maturity, I don't think I'll ever really take to it.

On the way home (we hadn't needed to consult each other to know that hooky time was over) I said, "The Thaxters want us at their cook-out tomorrow."

"I thought they'd had that ages ago," she said dully.

"No. It got rained out three Saturdays in a row." I suppose it went through both our minds that the last three Saturdays had been rainy, oppressive ones for her, too. The first in years that had not brought Mr. Wade to her side. "Will you come?" I said.

74

She drew one of those breaths that seemed to pain her, and said, "I think not, Anny. You go, and have fun."

"Michael's invited. In fact, it's only Michael that really is invited. They had to ask us to get him."

Madge, it was true, had stopped loitering on our doorstep since Michael spent most of his day immured in the attic, but I knew neither she nor her fly-by-night sister had altogether given him up. They were long-range prospectors.

"Don't be so prickly," Mother said to me.

"Well, it's true. They want him flushed, and who's to do it except us? Well, me."

"What of it?"

"Why don't you come? You might like it once you got there."

"I might." She paused, biting her lip. "No. I have work to do, anyway. If you'll get up early and get those beans in, Anny. They shouldn't wait much longer—"

She wouldn't be honest with me, and I thought to myself that it was going to be her fault if we never were close again. The old intimacy was gone, as I supposed it had to go when a child was no longer a child and a parent was a suddenly all-too-human being. But something else could surely take its place.

Only not if people aren't honest, I thought mulishly, forgetting how many barriers I myself had raised between us.

We were barely in the front door before Mother said, with a wretchedly thin attempt at nonchalance, "Any calls, Mrs. Halley?"

Filled with pity and contempt, I walked away, hearing Mrs.

75

Halley's, "The phone didn't ring once, dearie." I fancied her tone brimmed with ill-natured satisfaction and awareness, and when she called after me, "Anny, did you get my books?" I could scarcely bring myself to go back and give them to her.

If it had not been for Lenore's endless chatter dinner would have been prepared in total silence. What could we talk about? The cook-out Mother wouldn't go to? The House we could no longer dream of? The companionship we no longer had?

"You're awfully quiet," Mother said to me once.

I lifted my shoulders. "What's there to talk about?" I said derisively. "The Meaning of Life?"

"If you ask me," said Lenore, always on the defensive for Mother, "here's one nestling ready to be pushed from the nest when they get sassy out they go that's my system."

"Cheep, cheep," I said. "I don't know how to fly."

"Once you're pushed you'll fly all right."

"Oh, do stop it, both of you," Mother said, "or I'll do some flying myself."

After that, except for Lenore's low-key muttering, we were uncommunicative until dinner was on the table and the boarders gathered round it.

It's amazing how people will rally for the sake of face, or grace, in the public eye. Mother, lightly made up, wearing fresh blue gingham, presided at the head of the table with charm, finding something to say, something to reply, letting no awkward or telling silences fall. In my way—not as well— I, too, presented a calm and sociable front. And the food was excellent.

76

Mrs. Halley, laughing, eating like a trencherman, had apparently forgotten her own spiteful predictions. Mr. Beard, at the moment, was making no gloomy ones.

But Michael Vye was looking at Mother in a way he thought covert (except that I was more covert than he), and I knew one person was not misled by the careful façade we displayed.

CHAPTER *SIX*

The garden was still dewy when Tabu and I came into it
early on Saturday morning. Birds sang in the thickets, shot
forth and disappeared on their endless pursuit of food, flick-
ered around my little cat and eluded her, almost as if teasing.
There was a wonderful fragrance of greens and herbs fretting
the air, and a breeze blowing, strong enough to ruffle my
hair. I stood breathing it in with my eyes closed, taking a
pensive, sensuous pleasure in its freshness, in the way it flowed
coolly around me, touching my face, my hair, my bare legs.
It seemed to blow all sad, remembered things away, leaving
the world as new as morning.

"Oh, beautiful, beautiful," I murmured, and wanted to
throw my arms wide and call aloud. I felt impelled toward
some fugitive, flying promise of excellence or daring. My
eyes flew open and I tried to see more than my sight would
allow me, to breathe more deeply than my lungs would per-

mit. I strove for greater understanding than my mind would accord.

It was a sublime moment, dispersed at a shout from the newspaper boy, gone beyond recovery. (And yet perhaps not. Even today, when I remember that morning, the birds, the breeze, Tabu going scattered legged down between the rows of beans after a butterfly, that sense of young and ignorant exultance can touch me again, and I feel my destiny beckoning.)

"Got a bee in your bonnet, Anny?" yelled the newspaper boy.

"I'll put one in yours," I snapped at him.

"Oooh . . . I'm shook. I'll hafta lay down the rest of the day to recover from those words."

"May you never rise," I muttered, and kneeled to get at the beans. For a moment I was irritated with him for forcing upon me this reversion to age twelve. Then I forgot. The sky turned from pink to blue, the breeze eddied away, the birds were fewer. Peacefully I plucked the long green spears from their parent stems and dropped them in my basket.

Tabu, wearied by lack of success, flung herself down, white belly upward, legs flung out, head tipped back, eyes slitted. I looked at her and frowned with amusement and tenderness. She looked silly and unguarded and far too trusting.

"Do you realize you've lost all your jungle instincts?" I said to her. "You aren't a true feline any more. You're just a pampered domestic animal, relying on civilization and me to protect you. What if Mr. Beard is right, and there's a war, and all the people disappear? What if the jungle comes creeping back? What are you going to do then?"

79

She rolled to her side, fixed her great yellow eyes briefly on my face before the lids descended once again. It gave an impression of supreme ennui, and I decided that come what may, no jungle would find my cat napping.

Sitting back on my heels, I thought how peculiar it was that animals seemed to be equipped with everything they needed to survive, while with people it was just the other way around. It wasn't only listening to Mr. Beard (though I listened to him a good deal these days) that made me feel mankind was poised, with everything he needed to destroy himself, right on the edge of eternity. It was a chilling, heart-stopping conviction, more real than the certain knowledge of my own eventual death, but I didn't think about either one very often, or for long. How could I?

"Tabu?" I whispered. "Tabu? Go catch a mouse or climb a tree, but don't, I prithee, come troubling me." This aroused no response at all from her, but pleased and distracted me sufficiently so that I turned back to the beans.

It isn't enormities that are difficult to escape.

Some time later Michael Vye called to me from his attic window. "What have you there in your basket, Sister Anne?"

"Two dozen beans, a caterpillar, and a bobby pin," I called back happily.

"Like me to come down and help?"

"Oh, I would," I said.

When he came whistling out the back door, gaudy as a trout fly in his madras shirt and shorts, I got to my feet and stood waiting and watching with such candid bliss that he slowed, halted, and then remained at the edge of the garden looking at me, frowning slightly. Everything in his pose sug-

80

gested that another moment would see him gone, some muttered apology flung over his shoulder.

"It's a gorgeous morning," I said quickly. "I'm so happy, I'm . . . ecstatic. Did you ever get that way over the weather, Michael? Sort of goofy?"

He seemed to relax, and I pattered on like a magician seeking to divert suspicion with a flow of words.

"I was just saying to Tabu that I'm reasonably certain— don't you think that's simply another way of saying I'm absolutely sure? It is when Mrs. Halley says it, anyway—I am reasonably certain that whatever is going on in her mind isn't half as dizzy as what's going on in mine."

"Saints protect us, I hope not," he said, apparently lulled. He came into the garden down between the bean rows toward me, and I looked away, so as not to dismay or deter him.

A child, a child, remember that you are a child, I said to myself, and the echo went on and on in my head . . . child, child. I looked at him, an ingenuous smile in my disingenuous eyes, and said, "There's a heck of a lot of beans, Michael. Do you really mean to help?"

"Of course I do," he said, abruptly at ease with me again. If some lingering trace of the frown remained, I could interpret that. He was wondering what had got into him back there to imagine such improbable and improper things.

Five minutes later he'd forgotten all about it.

But I hadn't. I was facing, with sad certainty, the fact that I could never have him. I wouldn't be old enough quickly enough, he wouldn't be around long enough. If he'd been going to settle in the town, work here at his playwriting, if he were really a playwright instead of a chemist, then per-

81

haps I would have had sufficient season in which to change from child to woman. Given a decent course to run, I did not think it impossible to overtake him, and then beguile him into love for me. But I wasn't going to be given a run at all. I was frozen here in all the aspects of adolescence and he'd be gone before my race began.

Oh, unfair, unfair, I wept within my silence and my chatter. It is monstrously unfair—just for the lack of a year or two, to lose him, to be given no chance to win him. I felt like calling out, as Mother had the day before, *It is more than I can bear!*

"Michael," I said suddenly, "you came here on a one-way ticket. Why was that?"

"Didn't know how long I'd be here."

"Oh. You . . . do you know now?"

"Approximately. I'll be leaving sometime next week."

My heart plunged downward, hard as a stone, and I could feel the blood draining from my face, so that once again I had to avert my head. It's getting so I never dare look at him, I thought distantly, and then realized that soon there'd be no problem of that nature, or of any nature at all, in his presence. Soon I would only have to cope with his absence. "Oh, my love," I said soundlessly—like a woman, indeed— *"Oh, my love . . ."*

"As soon as that?" I said, when I could speak.

"It's getting on for fall, Anny. Hadn't you noticed?"

"I suppose I had. Lenore says the season's beginning to curl around the edges."

"Very descriptive. If I still had pretensions to the literary life, I'd ask her permission to use it. With a credit, of course. One should be careful about credits."

82

Now I looked up, heedless of danger in my concern for him. "You've given up, Michael?"

"As of this morning. As of when I got yawning to my feet and walked to the window and realized I'd rather pick beans with you than drag these paper characters off and onstage another minute."

There was no way to make a compliment out of that, and I didn't try. "Michael," I said, "are you absolutely sure?"

"I'm reasonably certain," he said with a grin, and then shook his head at me. "Don't look so desolate, Anny. All is not over. There are roads open to me yet."

"But you were so . . . so happy about it." I could not keep myself from sounding too bereft. Still, if it mattered, he wouldn't know it was not his literary career but his own dear presence I mourned.

For a moment I thought it did not matter. Just for a moment, heady and sweet, I thought, I'll throw myself into his arms and tell him how I love him, and beg him to wait for me. "Michael," I'll say, "look at me, please. You've never really looked at me if all you see is a thin, tall child with a tendency to stare. I'm *someone you could love*, in a year or two . . ."

I was so sure of what he was, so certain of how I felt, that I knew the wisest thing that he could ever do was to turn just then and really look at me. Only, I realized, he will have to look. I can't tell him, or beg him, or put it in words. I have to wait for him to see.

Look at me, Michael, I willed him in my mind. *Turn now and see me.*

He turned, and our eyes held. My heart was thudding. *See me, Michael . . . Look at me . . .*

"It's the darnedest thing," he said, "the way sometimes I think I'm talking with a kid, and then suddenly I think you're ageless. I've noticed this quality before in imaginative children."

"Have you?" I said wearily.

"Definitely. In fact, there was a character in this moribund play of mine that I was trying to make just such a person. Sort of like you, Anny, though actually I'd started the thing before I met you. Remarkable, when you come to think of it."

"Isn't it?" I turned back to the beans.

He had eyes, but he saw not, sensibility, but he felt not. Yet in no way did my love and admiration diminish. Nothing he did, or failed to do, would touch my love, I thought proudly. And truly. My first love, struck through as it was with images from books, ideals from poetry, and all the fancies that youth is heir to, was still, I think, the real thing. It took in its stride his failure to perceive me, my longings, my offerings.

The pile of cool, velvety beans mounted in the basket. The sun burned the dew away and fell upon us ever more hotly. I watched Tabu go down the garden and disappear. She'd gone to that low, leafy room that I had not been to since before Michael's arrival, and now it would be hours before I'd see her again.

"What are you sighing about?" Michael asked.

"I was? Oh, well, it was for another time, another place. A sort of secret place that Tabu and I shared, and that now I never go to any more."

"Why not?" he said gently.

"I . . . grew away from it."

84

He smiled a little, and then said, "It's the fate of secret places."

"Is it, Michael?"

"I think so. We put them behind us, or . . . outgrow them."

"Finding others, I suppose?" I did love this sort of conversation, and almost forgot my unhappiness in the prospect of one.

"Fewer and fewer," he said. "They either become harder to find, or—I prefer to think—less necessary."

"But if you had no place to hide when things got terribly sad, or just too *much*, why then you'd end up—" I broke off.

"You'd end up facing life," Michael said.

"All the time? I wouldn't put up with that."

"Nor would any of us, I suppose. Still, it's the direction one takes."

"Not me," I said firmly. "Not in our time."

"Our time. Aye, there's the rub." He nibbled reflectively on a bean.

"Mr. Beard says there's still a good chance he'll die of fission and not of age."

"He's a bitter man, and I don't like the way he sits in his inglenook, howling destruction. The way you and your mother put up with him is a wonder."

Mother had almost nothing to do with him, beyond the minimal landlady's attentions, but I didn't point that out. I decided that I couldn't point out, either, that I was learning from Mr. Beard. Staying with him, listening to his outcries and denunciations, when I might have been with Michael, or anyway in some less strident company, was teaching me something. But when I tried to explain, every word I thought of sounded priggish or toplofty: forbearance, understanding, tolerance. It was impossible to say just what I meant. But I could say, and did, that I found him a lonely old man and I didn't mind listening to him.

"He's sort of sweet, really. And his hands shake, and that touches me." I put my own hand to my heart. "I always feel like saying, 'There, there . . . don't worry.' Except, of course, that would infuriate him, because worrying is all he has, isn't it?"

Michael regarded me in a brooding way. "I begin to see," he said at length, "why I can't write that play. I'm not kind enough."

"Do playwrights have to be kind?" I asked innocently, and he burst into laughter.

"Anny, you're marvelous," he said. "A nonpareil."

Suffused with gladness, and, as usual, unequal to my joy, I said shrilly, "And here I was beginning to think you didn't care."

The words rang in the air, their gaucheness cruelly apparent, and I felt myself shrink inwardly, like an alarmed hedgehog. My eyes blurred with embarrassment, and I stirred the beans, as if searching through them.

Michael may not have had enough kindness to meet his own or that imaginary playwright's standards, but he had enough for mine. He said, with clear and apparent fondness, without a hint of disdain, "No one could help but care for you, Anny. You're an exceedingly likable girl."

Oh, I love you, I said silently, shakily. Michael, I love you *exceedingly*.

86

"Speaking of our times," he went on, making a fresh attack upon the beans, "there's a phrase of Pascal's I've always liked. We'd better move the basket on a way, Anny. This bush is denuded, utterly."

"Did Pascal have some comment to make on our time?" I asked, so grateful to him for putting the conversation back on its feet that I scarcely knew what I said. "I thought it was Nostradamus did the prophesying."

"Pascal was speaking for all time. He said, *Nous sommes embarqués*. Do you know what it means?"

"We are embarked?"

"Yes. Or, *We are on our way*. What he meant was, mankind is on its journey, and there is no going back. The phrase has a big, fateful sound. Gives me shivers, when I think of it. Shivers of awe."

"Because there's no going back?"

"And because of the way Pascal could *say* it like that, in three words. You know, whenever I get on an airplane, especially a jet, I remember those words. Think of it, Anny. As long as you're on the ground, your life is still within your control. You can get out, you can change your mind about where you're going, or whether you're going. But once that jet is in the air, you're on your way, with no power to make decisions, no choice of yea or nay. From there on it is all up to Fate, and that particular pilot's skill or fallibility. I think that's how Pascal saw us. On our way, but without determination, and no longer in control."

"You're as bad as Mr. Beard," I said without thinking. He looked so dashed that I began to search for appeasing words. "Actually, of course, I didn't mean—"

87

"Anny," he interrupted, "don't say what you mean and then pussyfoot around trying to unsay it. That's a bad habit to get into, understand?"

"Yes, Michael," I said meekly.

"You're right, of course. In my way, I'm as much a long-faced pessimist as Mr. Beard."

"You aren't long-faced at all."

"Long-spirited, then? Anyway, plagued by apprehension, visited by dreams of destruction . . ."

"Who isn't, these days? It's just that Mr. Beard doesn't see anything *but* gloom. Still, I think," I went on moodily, "that the people who are—who are *festive* about it all are worse."

"How's that?"

"Oh, you know. The world will end tomorrow, so let's raise hell today, and by all means let's go up in sables rather than securities. That sort of thing. I don't want everybody to be ants, but I get awfully bored by grasshoppers."

"You know, every now and then you sound so like your mother it's breathtaking."

"Do I?" I said, nonplused.

"Yes. That bit about sables and securities, just the sort of thing she'd say. She has a light sense of humor that puts things in perspective, you know?"

Since the bit about sables and securities was a product of the feather-brained Maureen Thaxter, I didn't know what to say, except yes, doesn't she?

"Anny," he said, as if arriving at a decision, "is there something wrong with your mother? Please don't think I'm prying just for curiosity's sake. I've grown very fond of—both of you. Perhaps if there was some way I could help—"

Dignity advised me to turn this offer aside and change the subject, but the chance to talk personally, intimately with Michael—even if the talk concerned my mother rather than me—was irresistible. Besides, he was a friend, had become one even in these short weeks. I could trust him.

"You mean you think she's changed?" I said tentatively, trying to find out what, exactly, he was thinking.

"Radically, I'd say. Don't tell me you haven't noticed it."

"Oh, yes, I've noticed," I said noncommittally.

"She was the essence of everything light-hearted. Sort of calmly gay in a way I never have quite seen before. I tell you, she's a wonder. I suppose you're used to it, Anny, but it's been a revelation to me. I come of a family that sees life sternly and sees it plain. Fine, good people, and I admire them, but it's uphill work to raise a laugh. There's no frivolity, no *trifling* with life. Your mother trifles with it all the time. Or did. One day—" He broke off, recollection smiling in his eyes.

I waited a moment before urging him on. It wouldn't do to turn sullen and indicate that I had no wish to speak of my mother's frivolity or her loss of it. In a way, I wanted to very much. Michael was wise, and he might think of some way we could help her. I didn't *want* my mother so changed and bleak-eyed, so utterly ungay.

But at the same time it did seem to me that the attention, especially Michael's attention, was always upon her, and I felt, though I still could not define how, some injustice in this situation. Surely parents were supposed to retire a little, if not

89

physically then at least temperamentally? Did they really go on and on this way, having emotions, taking the center of the stage? And if they did, what chance did green, crude, immature people, with none of their polish and less than half their years, have against them?

Lenore had called me a nestling, and I began to feel like one. Featherless and afraid, squawking my head off, while all eyes followed my mother's brilliant flight and her swift, fluttering descent.

"At this rate," I muttered to myself, "I'll never learn to fly."

"What's that, Anny?" said the sharp-eared Michael. "Fly where?"

I shrugged. "A bagatelle. I'm talking to myself to pass the time until you go on. You were saying that one day—"

"Oh. Yes. Well, one day your mother and I were downtown. I was helping her with the marketing, and we passed one of those little stands that kids make and sell lemonade on. The homemade sign, the big kitchen pot and ladle, the paper cups that have probably been dropped on the ground several times, and everything lukewarm. You know."

I nodded, knowing what was coming, and smiling in spite of myself. Michael was right, and Mother was a wonder.

"Well, do you know, she stopped, and very solemnly ordered two cups of that brew, one for her and one for me. God knows I'm sure the stuff was unsanitary, and anyway, I felt like a fool standing there beside that crate, with everybody going by looking. But"—he smiled, and his mouth twisted a little in fond amusement—"actually, I didn't feel like a fool. I only felt I should feel like one, because I would

90

have any other time. But your mother drank that cup of junk, standing there as if we were at a library tea, and I really got a big kick out of it. I guess it's that sort of thing that I mean. She just isn't like other people."

No, I thought, she isn't. She could do things like that, and play hooky, and never lose her high spirits, or even her temper, when heaven knew running a boarding house was enough to mangle most people's dispositions beyond repair. She wouldn't listen to Mr. Beard's program of annihilation, but she'd tend him when he was ill as if he were her child. By some alchemy she made Mrs. Halley's spitefulness mere whimsicality when she was around. After an hour of Lenore's voice I usually felt as if a woodpecker had gotten in my brain, but Mother went right on listening as if every word were vital to her well-being.

Thinking about her, listening to Michael, I experienced one of those moments of self-forgetfulness that came upon me from time to time unbidden.

"I can tell you what's wrong," I said to him, full of trust and reliance. "I can't tell you anything to do about it, and I don't see how you could think of anything either." I concluded on a rising note that practically asked him to challenge that.

"If you aren't betraying anything, I'd like to hear," he said. "Maybe we can think of something. Sometimes people who aren't directly involved can see more clearly."

"If I thought I were betraying anything," I said stiffly, "I'd hardly be speaking, would I?"

"Oh, Anny, act your age," he said, his voice indulgent.

And just what do you think that is? I wondered. Probably

if I asked him he'd say he never could tell a woman's age. It was the sort of thing— But no, I said to myself with a sigh. Michael Vye was not given to triteness. Trying to move away from the sore, futile topic, I said, "Mother's unhappy because her friend—you know Mr. Wade?"

Michael nodded. "I met him," he said tonelessly. "Is he the problem?"

"I guess so. I mean, yes."

"Not much of a—not much to him, is there?"

"More than you'd think," I said, remembering Mr. Wade's laughing arrival in a blizzard ("Oh, think nothing of it, Nan. I'd come to you through avalanches on a Saturday."), his steady eyes, his easy, "I'll take care of it," that time one of the boarders, now happily no longer bellowing with us, got drunk and started wrecking things. And he had taken care of it, by plain physical force and a strong voice. "He's slim, and he's quiet," I said, "but he's not a weakling. And he loves Mother. He really does."

"What's the hitch then? Is he married?"

"Oh, no. It's his mother. She's sort of—despotic."

"And he's sort of supine." His voice was hard.

"That doesn't sound like you, Michael."

"Who sounds like himself all the time?"

"You expect some people to. You expect some people will be themselves no mat—"

"Anny, don't go woolgathering. We were talking about your mother and her friend."

"I'm not sure I want to any more."

"Oh, come on. I'll be . . . I'll try not to be hard."

Reluctantly now, wishing I hadn't begun, I said, "She's

92

crippled, you see. His mother. She's the kind of mother who's had a hard life and now her son is making it up to her. You've read about them, or you ought to have. They're all over the books."

"That doesn't make them any more acceptable."

"Doesn't make them any more unusual, either, I guess. And she has this bad heart. I really don't see *how* Mr. Wade can cope with it. He wants to marry Mother, you know, but every time he talks to his mother about it, she swoons. I mean, really faints, and he has to call the doctor, and . . . Well, if it were your mother, you'd find it hard, too. I mean, unless you want to say, 'Go ahead and die, you old bat,' what can you do?"

"I'd know she wasn't for a minute going to die. That she was going to kick up a row and get over it. Period."

"I don't want to talk about it any more."

"You're right." He turned over the leaves of the last two bean plants, and said, "We've got them, one and all. That's quite a harvest, isn't it? How will we get them eaten?"

"We're going to freeze them."

"Your mother works all the time," Michael said, getting to his feet and picking up the basket.

I wanted to say, So do I. I wanted to say, Dry up and blow away. With a sigh I looked down the garden rows to see if there was any sign of Tabu, and then followed him toward the house. On the way I thought of something else. "Michael?" I said, trotting to get beside him. "What did the girl in your play look like?"

He gave me that affectionate, avuncular smile. "Like you. A gazelle of a girl."

93

"How old was she?"

"Oh, fourteen or so. I wasn't exactly sure of her age."

"Well, don't be too sure of mine," I muttered. And yet . . . I could not help smiling. Was I a gazelle of a girl? Such a pretty thing to be called.

CHAPTER *SEVEN*

"What're we going to do with all those tomatoes is what I want to know the cold room's full of them *and* the vines *and* look at all those over there on the sideboard I mean we just get well into the beans and look around and there're those tomatoes all over the place and I haven't even been able to get at the upstairs yet—"

"Lenore—" Mother began, always hopeful that this time a word would stem the tide.

"—you want the place shining all the time that's all right with me but if you drag me away from *up*stairs and make me come *down*stairs how *up*stairs is going to get polished is more than I can say or even the living-room windows which haven't been washed in a month or more—"

"Lenore!"

"Huh?"

"I didn't drag you away from upstairs," Mother said. "You came down. And I wish you would go back up, dear, and finish the polishing, because you're quite right, we're behind-hand with everything."

"You can say that again—" Lenore began, and I went deaf as effectively as if I'd turned off a hearing aid.

Michael had told me once that most people listen to words not their own with selective inattention. That was, they heard partially, they picked up references to themselves or their interests, failed to hear anything that would displease or upset them, overlooked what you had to say about your-self, and finished only half aware of having been in a conver-sation at all. I sort of thought he was right. Even when I was determined to listen—as, for instance, in my discussions with Mr. Beard—I invariably wandered off on some matter of my own (mentally, that is), returning once in a while, like someone checking the roast, just to be sure he was all right. I was not proud of this, but didn't seem to be able to do anything about it.

But selective inattention was no answer to the volubility of Lenore. Nothing but total deafness would do, and that's what I employed as I washed and sorted and cut beans.

Michael is leaving, I thought. Pretty soon Michael will not be here. I had not had much experience with missing people. The only important person who had ever left my life was my father, and I hadn't missed him much at the time. It was as the years went on that I realized some deeply-needed being was not with me. I was more conscious of his absence than I had ever been of his presence.

Now the other man I loved and needed was going, and I
96

did not think that he'd come back. Out of a desperate need to protect myself from the pain that his absence would bring, I fashioned a plan for the future. Since a life that did not include him ever again was unconfrontable, and since he would not come back here (I didn't know how I knew this, but I knew it), then I would go to him. He would be gone, but I would grow to meet him, shaping myself to his future, and one day I would leave this town and go to where he was.

I saw myself, svelte, self-assured, exquisitely groomed, a gazelle of a young woman wearing a soft, mysterious smile that would turn people's heads, and they would say, seeing me, What secret, perfect thought is in her possession? But, on my way to Michael, I would not see them.

I would call him on the phone. "Michael Vye? This is Anny Miles. I don't know whether you'll remem—"

"Anny!" he'd cry out, in a ringing tone of pleasure. "Remember you, Anny? What a ridiculous thing to say. Why, meeting you altered my whole life." Snapping beans, my eyes unfocused with prevision, I wondered *how* meeting me would have altered his whole life. Oh, well, there were any number of ways a person could affect somebody else. No need to be over-precise. "Anny, where are you?" he'd say insistently.

"I'm right here in your city, Michael. And I was just wondering—that is, if you aren't too busy—"

He'd laugh and say again how foolish I was, and whatever he was doing would be put aside so he could come to meet me. I'd arrange for us to meet in a big hotel lobby, a place where there'd be many people. He would come in (I'd be there before him) and stand looking around, with that puzzled frown I knew so well.

Would he look just the same? Nearly. I added a few gray hairs, tenderly etched a line here and there. But, essentially, Michael, as he was now, because I couldn't bear for him to change. His searching eyes would cover the lobby, pass over me, return, hover, start away again, and then, finally, irrevocably, come to rest on my face.

He'd come forward, as if mesmerized, his hands reaching for mine. "It can't be," he would say. "And yet, of course, it is. Only Anny, Anny, what have you done?"

"I've grown up," I'd say simply, without evasion. "And now I've come to you."

"Yes," he would whisper. "Yes, I see. This is how it had to be."

"There was no other way, Michael. I knew it the first time I saw you."

"I must have known it, too. Without knowing, I must have known." And then he would laugh exultantly, in the manner of a man who has found his fate, and sober suddenly, as a man who has found, at last, his love.

"Anny!"

I jumped and cried out nervously at Lenore's voice.

"I'm trying to get these here beans away from you I mean you maybe don't have anything to do except moon around but your mother and I are working if you'd just let go of them—"

My arms had encircled the large bowl of beans (which I had apparently long since finished snapping into two-inch lengths), and I sat there as if protecting it. I felt reassured, at peace. There was no reason, really, why my plan shouldn't work, if not in detail, then in its general scope. Adolescence

98

is a self-eliminating condition and every day brought me closer to the finale of that stage in my life. When it was finished, I would arise and go to Michael Vye.

On the periphery of my consciousness a question posed itself. Perhaps he would be married? It glanced away from me, weightless as a dandelion clock. The thought was not admissible. It had no place in my dreams, so I gave it none. Michael would be then as Michael was now. Only I would be different. And no matter where he was, no matter how far, *I would come from the next world, Michael, when it is time to be with you.* It was a promise I was making, not to myself, but to Michael who might one day love me.

"Mrs. Miles, she's guarding those beans as if they were a litter and at least if she won't help she could let loose of them so I could package them couldn't she she just *sits* there—"

I got dreamily to my feet and said to Lenore, "I thought you'd gone upstairs."

"That'll be enough from you Miss Pert if you're not gonna help your mother then somebody has to and its perfectly plain you aren't gonna sitting there moping and mooning and making faces to yourself—"

"Lenore, *please*," said Mother, and then, "Anny, for goodness' sakes, if you can't be of more practical use, why don't you go up and sit in the window seat?"

"What's all the fuss about?" I said. "I'm willing to help. Delighted, in fact. What shall I do?"

"Oh, I give up," said Lenore, and stomped off to finish the upstairs.

"What's her trouble?" I asked Mother, who scowled and

99

wouldn't answer. So I got to work, filling the white containers with beans, wishing I could write on them, "Michael Vye picked these."

"Why are you in such a dandy mood?" Mother asked suddenly. "Not that I don't relish it, but why? Can two people fit?"

I thought quickly, nodded, and said, "Sure, except you won't. I'm thinking about the cook-out. It's going to be a steak one, not shish kabobs, and the weather's decent at last and I can wear my new dress . . ."

"Darling, you don't get out often, do you?" Mother said, her voice strained and unhappy. "I suppose it's that you stay here and work so willingly that I forget it isn't what a girl your age should be doing. Heaven knows I don't want it to be this way. I want you to have friends and go out, I want you to have fun."

"There's nothing wrong with my life. I have a fine time."

"Doing what? Playing solitaire with Mrs. Halley? Listening to old Cassandra Beard day in and day out, and once in a while for a real treat having that self-conscious young man help you with the beans?"

"Mother!" I gasped. "What are you talking about? Why, Michael is . . . Michael Vye is the *least* self-conscious person I've ever known. You said yourself that he has dozens of interests—that first day you met him."

"Well—I guess he has. But they're all *his* interests. I mean—even when he's showing all that lovely concern for people I get the feeling that it's gratifying his own ego to *be* concerned. Maybe I'm not making myself clear."

"You certainly aren't, and besides, you're wrong. He

100

never thinks about himself at all. He's constantly thinking about other people. And not to satisfy his own ego. Why, he's worried to death about you—"

"About me?" Mother said sharply. "Why should he worry about me?"

"Oh, Mother—" I moved uneasily. "No reason, really. You don't look exactly feverish with joy lately, you know. Anyone who liked you would worry." She looked at me steadily, and I blurted, "Well, Mother, what *do* you think of life these days, exactly?"

Her glance fell. "It isn't Paradise Regained, if that's what you mean. Only I don't see what call Mr. Vye has to concern himself."

"Now, that's where you're being unfair," I said. "He concerns himself because he likes you. He likes you very much indeed, and if I were you, I'd be proud. I wouldn't go around calling him that self-conscious young man—"

"I don't go around calling him that. I just said it to you. I take it back, if it troubles you. Besides, I didn't mean it the way you took it. I meant pretentious, not conceited."

"I don't see how you could *arrive* at such a totally wrong conclusion. You're usually so good at people, at sizing them up."

"Perhaps because I'm a little uneasy with him, Anny. I don't know. I'm sure I'm wrong, if you're so sure." She studied me again and said, "Surely you and he don't discuss — No, of course you don't."

I was relieved that she answered herself, because I would not have known what to say if she'd put it to me directly. Yet I was not rueful at having spoken of her with Michael,

101

whose gentle affection could never take advantage, who would never pry from idleness. In the past, the only person I'd ever had to talk seriously with, or take my problems to, was Mother. If Michael Vye hadn't been here now, there would have been no one, since the person I always went to was herself a problem.

And in a way I either wouldn't or was unable to define, it did not disturb me to find Mother wasn't too fond of Michael. In my youthful arrogance I would have had him unloved, unwanted by anyone save me, and then, I thought, I would love him even more. I would make up to him for the world's indifference, I would comfort and sustain him, and he would turn to—

"Anny, look," Mother said, and had to lift her voice. "Go upstairs, will you? I have problems of my own, and you're beginning to make me nervous mooning around here and getting in the way. I can finish up faster if I'm alone."

"Maybe if you told me your problems," I said shrilly, "we could talk them out, or something. You go around keeping everything to yourself, and it's impossible for anyone to *reach* you."

Confide in me, I demanded mutely, in much the same way that I had pleaded, *Look at me* a few hours ago in the garden.

Like Michael, Mother was inaccessible to my unspoken plea, and I had a moment of wishing to renounce them both. They wanted nothing I had to offer.

If I could barter five years of the end of my life, I thought bitterly, and have them now, if I could be twenty right this minute in a devil's bargain, oh, how I would make it! Before they had time to observe me I'd be gone, and not to Michael. To my own life, lived in my own way, and I would never beg a boon, aloud or in silence, of anyone again, nor offer myself to be spurned ever again.

"Anny," Mother said, putting her hand on mine, "try to understand. I can't talk about—things. I can't add my troubles to yours. Don't you see?"

"I do not have a trouble," I said stiffly, looking at her hand and waiting for her to remove it. "Not one little trouble of my own. Or anything else of my own, for that matter."

"Including a mother?" she said gently.

"If you wish to put it that way."

She walked away, turned, and came back to sit across from me. "I've been very selfish. I didn't realize how hurt you are."

"Hurt about what?" I said. "What should I be hurt about? Nothing's happened to me."

As if I hadn't spoken, she said, "People get absorbed, Anny, in their own little section of the puzzle. They get so tied up trying to find the lost piece, or fit the piece that *must* go in but somehow won't, that they forget it's only a corner, and that other people are trying to work it out, too. I guess this sounds silly—"

"Sort of," I said unforgivingly. "After all, life *isn't* a puzzle."

"No? Well, it's a habit of mine, trying to oversimplify."

I know your habits. I used to love them, love them . . . "I didn't mean to sound stuffy," I said with difficulty. "I'm just tired of spooking around as if I were transparent, or something. Do you know the only person who *looks* at me—I

103

mean, who sees somebody is there in front of him that's made of flesh and blood and has something to offer, is Mr. Beard? Well, I'm sorry, but I can't make a career of Mr. Beard. I mean, I like him, but after all. And you and Michael . . . you act as if I were somebody you *remembered*, not somebody walking around in front of you and talking and maybe being worth talking to—"

"Michael?" Mother said.

"Yes, Michael, Michael, Michael . . . who is not self-conscious, or pretentious, or anything but the most wonderful person who ever lived, except blind and deaf as a bat, just the way you are."

I could hear myself becoming incoherent, telling all I'd meant to keep my own, and could not stop. All the rejection, loneliness, bewilderment of the summer crowded forth and found tongue as I berated equally Mother, Michael, the boarders, the people who'd stolen The House, Miss Fillmore, and my lost father. When, at last, I ran down into silence I sat shaken, just this side of being actively sick, and dully convinced that I had now so irretrievably ruined everything that continuing to live could be only a meaningless gesture.

I kept thinking how happy I had been in the garden in the morning, but had no recollection of why.

"I've been very selfish," Mother said again. As if saying it would make her less so. "I know saying that doesn't make me less so," she went on, and I glanced at her quickly. Here she'd go for weeks not hearing a thing I said, and then she'd take the words right out of my mind. "I'm not reading your mind," she said, continuing to read it. "It's a self-evident

104

fact. Admitting a fault does not erase it. Still, it's a step, isn't it, Anny?"

She waited, and I dipped my head slowly, like a convalescent.

"It's a funny thing," she went on, "how all my life I've disliked people who inflict their very personal miseries on those around them, and here I've been guiltier than anyone I can call to mind. When I consider how unhappy people bore me, it's really too much—"

"Unhappy people *bore* you!" I burst out. "That's a terrible thing to say."

"I don't mean unhappiness that has a reason and a terminal point. I mean creeping, day-to-day misery that won't be comforted and infects everything about it and adores being unhappy. The way I've been."

"But if you have a reason—"

"Anny, something you'll learn in time, or perhaps have learned now, in which case"—she smiled wryly—"I will have taught you a truth and served some purpose with this—this despond of mine. Where was I? Something you'll learn is that the world will put up with unhappiness just so long. If you are bereaved, or heartbroken, or just plain blue, people will feel for you and sympathize most sincerely— for a while. After that, you're on your own. You can mourn and moan the rest of your life, if that's all you see to do, but you can't expect other people to go along with you. They get tired of it, and they have every right to. Just as you've gotten tired of me."

"I haven't gotten tired of—"

105

"Excuse me, Anny. I meant, tired of my miseries. I guess I've become so self-pitying that I talk that way even when I don't mean to. But *that's* the sort of thing I mean. I'm boring to you and believe me I'm boring to myself, too. I've been floundering around in this morass, and I guess expecting you to cluck and say, Poor Mother, how did she get in there? But never lose your patience. It's asking too much."

"How *did* she get in there?"

The room became very still. Then, with a distant smile, Mother said, "Self-help, mostly." She clasped her fingers together, looked at them for a long time, then up at me with an air of decision. "You see, Anny . . . I told Mr. Wade either to . . . either to marry me, or stay away." She stopped, breathing tiredly, and I said nothing.

"You can see what his decision was," she resumed slowly. "The trouble is—I keep hoping. I mean, I *have* kept hoping. Hope is a terrible deterrent to action, I find. And so . . . you've had to suffer, too. And I'm sorry."

I could find nothing, nothing at all to say. I'd asked for her confidence, I'd demanded to be spoken to like an adult, and now I didn't know how to react like one. If I had no one to go to but Mother, she, since Mr. Wade was gone, had no one but me. It looked as if we weren't going to be much good to each other. I didn't know how to speak to her about Mr. Wade. I assured myself that I understood how, driven and desperate, she could propose to him, just to have it settled one way or the other. Only I couldn't understand, and felt hot with shame for her rejection. Mortified for and by her, I could say nothing, now that she'd told me the problem I'd asked to help with.

106

And it was clear that she either hadn't listened to or was going to overlook my emotional outburst concerning Michael. Whether because she considered it an overexcited reaction, signifying little, or because she just didn't wish to see the consequences of taking it seriously, I couldn't tell.

Straightening, lifting her chin a little, she said, "Let me give you more of my hard-won knowledge, the sort that comes from age and not from books. There are times when the *only* thing to do is start from right here. You may want to go back and reword things and recant and have it all to do over more wisely than before, but you simply cannot do it. So . . . no repining, see? You say to yourself, that's that, and this is this, and here is where I start from."

Was she, after all, talking about Michael? Not using his name, but telling me what to do about him?

"Forgetting everything?" I began to grow calm. I had a lot of faith in my mother still. If she told me we could say that's that and this is this, why, then, no doubt, we could. A fresh start at fifteen may sound a little silly, but I sometimes think that those are the years when fresh starts, again and again, are most necessary. Because you make so many mistakes, I suppose.

Sitting there in the kitchen with Mother, I thought I'd even be willing to renounce Michael, if it would make her the way she had been in the old days. That the one would not necessarily follow, in fact had little at all to do with, the other did not occur to me. I was in a propitiating mood. I'll do this for you, Lord, then you do that for me. Between my love for Michael and my great desire to have again the old relationship with my mother, I veered like a person in a swing boat, in a gigantic arc with two resting points, and, between, nothing but the dive and upsurge of rushing from one pole to the other.

I said to myself, "*Je suis embarqué*. Not getting anywhere, of course, but, oh, so *embarqué* . . ."

Mother's watchful eyes were on me. I met their steady regard, smiled a little, feeling diffident, and said at length, "Well . . . what now?"

"Now the beans, I suppose. I'd hate to have Lenore come down and find we still haven't done them."

"The trouble with you," I said in a light, nearly natural tone, "is that you let people intimidate you."

"Oh, I don't know about that. When did you last tell anyone off? Except possibly Tabu?"

We—the word would be chaffed, I suppose—one another in a reasonable facsimile of the accustomed way, and in an oddly detached fashion I felt tender toward the two of us, rather as I felt toward Mr. Beard when, for the sake of our growing friendship, he tried to be optimistic about man's world.

When Lenore came back, we were beginning preparations for the evening meal. Mother, assembling a meat loaf, her deft fingers moving quickly, said, "I suppose I could have made another Sally Lunn for Michael. He hasn't had one in over a week."

I interpreted this as a peace offering. "You could to it tomorrow," I said. "Anyway, Michael won't be here for dinner. He and I are going to Thaxters', remember?"

"True." Tossing spices in the bowl, Mother sighed and said, "I get so tired of the way people eat. Give them a good meal today, and they're around again tomorrow asking for more. There's no end to it."

I laughed. "Why don't you come with us, then? Lenore would do dinner tonight, wouldn't you, Lenore?"

"Not for you Miss Nose-in-the-air . . . but if you want to go to the affair Mrs. Miles I'd be glad to take over glad to—"

Mother hesitated, and then with a decisive air, said, "Oh, of course I will. I'd be happy to, Anny. And you're an angel, Lenore. The dinner's quite simple, really. Look, I'll show you."

They bent over the menu together, Lenore looking conscientious, and Mother quite convincingly cheerful, like someone who has just taken a tonic the doctor has assured her will work.

CHAPTER *EIGHT*

There are people—Mr. Beard was one of them—dedicated to the proposition that life is a tribulation somehow to be gotten through but never to be enjoyed, and there are others unable to sustain misery no matter what the cause. My mother was one of these.

Poverty, overwork, lack of leisure or freedom scarcely touched her good humor at all. Sometimes I thought she was courageously overlooking them, and sometimes it seemed she simply didn't realize that these were her daily portion. Illness, mine or her own, troubled her only until she was sure that this time it was nothing serious. She never read anything but homemaking magazines, so the world ran ruinward without her knowledge, and her method with afflictions close to home was to do what she could and then get out of the way.

I had seen her struck down and helpless only twice, and

110

the first time I scarcely remembered. After my father died I was conscious of a great loss, not of himself but of my mother's bright, pervasive spirit. When I wept in the night it was not for his familiar bulk, his low and comforting voice, but for fear of the chill and despair that filled our house and my mother's eyes.

I have no clear idea of how long that lasted, but I do remember the moment when her eyes seemed to clear, and look at me again, and she smiled. It had snowed in the night, and I waked to a white world and the exciting sound of snow shovels and soft chunking chains on passing automobiles and the milkman stamping his galoshes on the back porch. I looked at the drifts piled on my window sill and forgot that for me the world had gone empty and gray.

Dashing downstairs to dress by the stove—it was early and the rest of the house was still cold—I found Mother making oatmeal. The line of her body was stooped, and she didn't turn as I came into the kitchen.

"Mama!" I called. "Mama! It's *snowing*."

"I know, dear. Isn't that nice?" There was no inflection in her voice and still she did not turn.

"I wish it would just keep falling all white this way and pile up and pile up . . . white as polar bears or white foxes. Mama, *don't* you wish it would just keep snowing and never stop at *all?*"

Still she stirred the oatmeal, and I was resigned to talking to myself, when suddenly she spun around and grabbed me close and said against my hair, "Of course I do, Anny. Forever and ever."

I pulled away so that I could see in her face, and a stone

111

rolled off my heart. The blue remembered gaze was once again as I remembered it—or close enough to suit a chilled and lonely child. She was seeing me, and caring about what I said, and laughing with me over the snow.

"It's early," she said. "Let's put the oatmeal at the back of the stove and go for a walk. What do you say?"

I whooped with joy and was warned only lightly of sleeping boarders, and from that day on if Mother suffered it was not evident to me.

When Mr. Wade left she sank, in a different way but the same direction, nearly as far as she had that other time. Only now I was aware of every passing hour, conscious all the time of the lost harmony and sparkle that had made insignificant the drudgery of our lives. Aware of her despair— and her defection—I certainly was, but as the first time I had been too young to comfort her, this time I was too preoccupied with Michael Vye. I think we only fail the people who matter in our lives, and these we fail continually, not through design but helplessness.

So, with no word from Mr. Wade, no help from me, Mother endured those bitter weeks and then because it was her nature and inescapable, she looked around and found the sun falling through the kitchen window, reflecting off a blue bowl on the sideboard. She saw Tabu strutting sleekly through the door, heard Lenore and me snapping at each other as usual but urging, in one voice, the Thaxters' cookout on her. Or she looked in her daughter's face, and felt needed. She found, in other words, life going on as before, and she awake again to face it. Once she'd admitted that,

112

she could no more suppress her own pleasure and interest in the business than a tree can hold down the rising saps of spring.

Remember and regret she might, but she could not mourn any longer, and as I went upstairs to sit in the window seat awhile before dressing, I was wishing for something more of her in me. I was losing the person who mattered most to me in the world (next to Mother, I added punctiliously—but in my deepest heart still put Michael first), and I hadn't Mother's unflagging spirit to see me gracefully through the loss.

Already I felt what it was going to be like, passing the attic door and knowing he was not up there working on his play—or, more likely, reading. I was missing him very much before the day of leave-taking was even set.

I could hear him up there now, walking to and fro in a patterned stride. It occurred to me that he must be packing. Six steps toward the bureau, a pause, six steps toward the bed. Yes, this was the beginning of his departure. I drew up my knees and clasped them close, resting my head on their bony surfaces, and realized that I was not so much unhappy as stiff and dull.

I listened to his footsteps going back and forth, listened to Tabu's late-afternoon hymn, and the breeze stirring the old summer-toughened leaves of the sycamore, and I thought that this lassitude I felt in mind and body was a sort of resting up for the real ordeal that lay ahead, when everything was going to remind me that he was gone. Words were going to hurt, and recollections. The garden would seem

113

empty. I supposed that for a while the world would be like the garden—empty no matter who was in it.

I had read so much that I knew in advance, without ever having felt it, the pain of this kind of loss. I knew, too, that this time I would not be able to burrow into my books and forget. One by one the secret places were disappearing, the escape hatches closing. It was an aspect of growing up that I hadn't considered until recently, but it seemed that Michael was right, and like it or not, willy-nilly, you ended up facing life.

All right, then, I thought. All *right*. If I have to face it, I will do it on my own terms. I will suffer, because there's no escaping it, but meanwhile I'll be growing older—there's no escaping that, either—and as I grow each moment will bring me closer to the time when I am my own person. Free, grown, with no need of escape hatches. Who couldn't face life if he was on his own, answerable to no one? I said this to myself very seriously as I planned to suffer and then to recover from suffering, to grow and then to be suddenly grown, to miss Michael and then go to him and find him waiting. As if I were drawing routes on a map. As if the map were guaranteed against misprints or alteration.

We met in the hall shortly before five, ready to set out for Thaxters'. Michael wore black shorts, knee socks, a blue hopsack shirt. His dark hair gleamed, his smile was very quick, and he looked pleased, even exhilarated. Not over the cook-out, I thought. Over what, then? I started to ask, and then Lenore came out of the dining room, talking to herself, and when she found she had an audience, to us.

"The yellow casserole's got a crack in it did you do that

Anny I went all over West Hell finding that casserole in the first place and now it's got this crack in it oh well what's the diff it'll be all right for a while yet I just hate having nobody say anything to me when things happen like that it's the best one we have you know I was thinking this might be the night to poison Mrs. Halley if I can get away with it that is—" She broke off, staring up as Mother came down the stairs wearing her lime-green cotton.

"Well look at that will you it seems to me Anny could've got just one new dress and you got one too Mrs. Miles not that you don't look adorable but after all there's justice in things but no everything's for the kids these days and grownups just have to make do with leftovers if you ask me there's some around here could think about other people once in a—"

"Lenore!" Mother said, taking her by the arm. "Stop for a second, will you? Look, come on back in the kitchen and I'll check to be sure everything's in order. Not, of course, that it won't be, but still—" They went down the hall. "Back in a second," Mother called to us.

Michael was shaking his head. "That woman must have a machine in her larynx. No ordinary human equipment could manage."

I didn't answer. I was looking down at my dress, one of the two I'd had in more than two years. A red-and-blue plaid with a ruffle around the hem. A rather old-timey dress, I'd thought when I bought it. I felt sweet in it. At least, I had until Lenore's outburst. When had Mother had a new dress? I couldn't remember, but resented, deeply, Lenore's criticism. She'd made me look selfish in front of Michael. I

115

hate her, I said to myself, and immediately took it back. She was not that important to me, the old magpie. It wasn't hatred I felt for Lenore. It was nothing stronger than antipathy. At the moment the antipathy was very, very strong.

"Oh, come on, Anny," Mother said, returning. "Haven't you gotten used to Lenore yet?"

"I doubt if I ever will."

"As I pointed out to her, I don't outgrow my clothes, and you do. Children need more things than adults do."

"Anyway, that green's gorgeous," Michael said to her. "You look like an *apéritif*."

I wanted to walk away and leave them both, but, since that was impossible, settled for a chilly silence, which they, as we strolled toward Thaxters', were talking too much to notice.

"Are you hungry?" Michael asked her.

"Starved."

"Me, too. 'There are four important things in life,' said Mme. de Montespan. 'One of them is dinner and I forget the other three.' "

Mother burst into laughter, and Michael said, "That sounds good. To hear you laugh."

"I wonder what the other three were," said Mother, missing the point on purpose.

Michael, sounding chastened, said, "It's remained a mystery." They walked a few steps in silence. "Tell me, do you ever get down to Boston?"

"Never."

"Why not?"

"Well, sometimes."

"Why did you say never?"

116

Silence again, and then she said, "I'm not sure. Look, there are two cars turning in to Thaxters'. This must be quite an affair—"

I was lagging farther and farther behind, wanting them to notice and turn and call me to them. When they did not, my heart began to thud and my footsteps dragged heavily. It was like being forgotten. *Like?* I said to myself. It *is* being forgotten. The blood burned in my cheeks and I looked around with an underlying desperation, as if there'd be some place to run if I could find it. Except that of course I couldn't run. I'd have to follow them, hurry to catch up if we were to arrive together at the party.

They turned at the gate, not looking back, and were gone. By chance the street was empty for a moment and I stood absolutely still, staring at the privet hedge, feeling alone, bereft, betrayed. Completely out of proportion to what had happened— they had merely gone in a neighbor's gate a few steps ahead of me, and part of me knew it perfectly well—I felt cruelly, deliberately misused, frozen out by the two people who most of all should have cherished and warmed me. I was conscious, too, of an irrational, detestable pleasure in this anguish. Everything I felt lately was excessive. The joy of this morning, the nerveless lethargy of this afternoon. Now this burning sense of desertion. Nothing mild or moderate, nothing I could handle.

I stood, feet nailed to the ground, head swimming, wondering what was going to happen now. When Mother reappeared at the gate and looked inquiringly down the street, I jerked like a marionette and started toward her, a thousand bitter words crowding to my tongue.

"Darling," she said, "what happened? I looked around, and there you weren't."

"I . . . had a stone in my shoe."

I waited for her searching eyes to find out my misery, waited for her consoling words which I would turn away at first. She wasn't going to comfort me as easily as she'd left me. There's nothing wrong, I would say. Nothing at all. I'm fine, and I don't know what you're talking about. Gently to start with, and then with increasing anxiety she would try to find what had happened, how I had been hurt, and it would slowly be borne in upon her how cruel it had been to go laughing off with Michael, not even noticing that *I was left behind.*

"Is it out now?" she said.

"Out?" I cried, as if prodded on a bruise. "Is what out?"

"Dear, the stone. In your shoe. Did you get it out?"

"Hey! What's keeping you two?" Michael bounded through the gate and toward us. "Come on, ladies. There's food in that there back yard. I'm maniacal with hunger and ready to eat boiled telephone wire."

"Oh, dear," said Mother. "I don't believe the Thaxters serve it."

He seemed to find this really amusing, and they turned to go back. This time Mother took my hand and steered me along between them, so that we arrived among the Thaxters and their guests looking a happy trio. Anyway, a solid trio.

Maureen, in stretch pants and a pink ruffly shirt, was at the barbecue pit, helping her father turn steaks. She turned, looked at Michael, said, "Oooh," and let the long fork dangle down uselessly.

"Hey," said her father, turning, too. He spied us and waved. "Oh, good. You made it."

They came forward, Maureen's eyes flashing at Michael, Mr. Thaxter smiling at Mother and calling to his wife to come meet the newcomers. We were absorbed by the party. The music from a phonograph, the sizzling of the steaks, the swelling tide of voices engulfed and swept us apart. Madge came up to me and said, "Anny, come over here . . . there's a bunch of kids from school." Grimly acquiescent, without grace, I went with her, thinking how not too long ago I had wanted Madge to sponsor me with her particular bunch of kids from school.

I didn't want to be surly and crabbed. I wanted, terribly, to be able to rise above my suffering and smilingly charm those around me. I wanted, at the very least, to be a decent sport. But I sat in a daze, stiff and unfamiliar, fostering my fate as an unpopular girl at school. ("Anny Miles? Don't ask *her*. A disposition like ground glass and a face like the side of a glacier.")

My afternoon's dream of victorious maturity seemed a small candle in this great forlornness. I tried to return to it, telling myself how I would look, and smile, and one day call Michael to my side with a word. I tried to picture his face as he came toward me across the hotel lobby, his eyes bright with surprise and awakening love.

Useless . . .

There was no future, there was only here and now, and even that had scarcely begun. I wished I were home with Tabu, or listening to Mr. Beard, or even playing solitaire with Mrs. Halley. I wished I were dead, reserving, as we do,

119

the right not to mean it. I wished I were anywhere but where I was, here, utterly separated from Michael present or Michael future, with an entire evening ahead of me that had somehow to be gotten through.

With a sigh, I decided I'd better begin and turned an awful smile upon a boy sitting next to me. "Nice party, isn't it?" I said icily.

"The bee's knees," he replied, and a moment later had slithered off like a newt.

There was a big wooden table set up, where we sat when we'd served ourselves to steak, corn, salad, rolls, and iced tea. It all looked very good, and I wished I wanted any of it. Like my other wishes, it was no go. I put as little as possible on my plate, wondered if I could throw it in the bushes without being noticed, decided I couldn't, and sat down.

By now people had given up disturbing me, so I sat and listened to the conversation, which was like that of Babel, as it usually is at a cook-out. I noticed that my head was beginning to ache, and almost welcomed that as a tangible reason for my intangibly horrible feelings. If I was sick, I was sick, and no blame could be attached to me for my behavior.

Attentive to the increasing pain in my temples, I suddenly became aware of Mr. Thaxter's loud voice. He was slightly stoned, which was the only time he ever got to talk loudly—or much at all in his household of women.

"I tell you, Vye," he was saying, leaning across the table and shaking an ear of corn at Michael to emphasize his words, "this is the Age of Conformity. Conformity, and you can't get around it any more than I can. You may think you don't, but you've *got* to conform. If you don't, you'll never get on

120

the conveyor belt, and if you don't get on the conveyor belt, you'll never get to the place where the money rolls out, and if you don't get there, O my soul, then what have you been fighting for?"

I glanced at Michael, who was smiling—at the "O my soul," I thought to myself.

"Now, take my daughters," Mr. Thaxter went on. "*They're* conforming. They think they are nonconformists and lord knows what they're conforming *to* is a drizzling mystery to me, but when you come right down to it, they conform. They wouldn't dare not to. They do what all their friends do—buy, buy, buy. Buy the first thing they see. And the second, and the third. But there's nothing *original* about it—"

"Dad!" said Madge and Maureen, and, "Really, dear," said Mrs. Thaxter.

But the father of the barbecue looked at Michael and said, "They consider themselves daring and defiant—they think they're more reckless than my generation had the guts to be. But actually they're just spendthrifts on a bigger scale. And *that's* because my generation still doesn't have any guts and can't stop them. Mine wasn't the Lost Generation, you know. We came after them. We're the Gutless Generation." He dropped the ear of corn on the ground, stared at it morosely for a moment, and then said to Michael, "Don't you agree? You girls hush. *I'm* talking now. Don't you, Vye?"

"Do I think it's the Age of Conformity?" Michael said prudently.

People were listening to them now, and I knew how Michael liked to be listened to. I didn't think less of him for it; it was just something I'd known since that first evening at

121

dinner. I supposed now that it was one of the reasons—probably, I decided dismally, the main reason—he talked to me so much. Not because I was myself, but because I was a good listener.

"Well—okay, answer that, then," Mr. Thaxter said, "if you don't dare answer the other."

"I think of this as the Age of False Modesty," Michael said, sounding pleased with himself. "The war heroes won't display their ribbons, the Phi Beta Kappas won't wear their keys, the doctors won't even hang their diplomas on the office wall any more. I, myself, am the possessor of a Phi Beta Kappa key, but being a child of my age, naturally wouldn't be caught dead wearing it."

"But you just told us about it," Maureen said on a bursting giggle, as if finding him out.

"Ah, but that, too, is the spirit of the age. Remember, I said *False* Modesty. How many times do you read in a newspaper about some politician whose many philanthropic activities have been kept from press and public alike? Or the profile in a slick magazine of a slick public figure who refuses to discuss his war record so it is not generally known that he is the holder of the Distinguished Service Cross? If we haven't already seen it, we undoubtedly will see photographs in *Life* of a movie star snapped in the act of secretly handing a check for an undisclosed $100,000 to the director of the Handicapped Children's League. Of course it's what we all want, to be discovered doing our unobtrusive good acts."

"Oooh, I think you're terrible," Maureen said dotingly.

"In all false modesty," said Michael, "I agree."

122

Mr. Thaxter bellowed with amusement. I looked at the other guests, most of whom were eying Mr. Thaxter and Michael expectantly, waiting for more. Then my glance fell upon Mother. She was laughing, too, and looking at Michael with an expression of light-hearted possessiveness. It meant nothing. Only that he'd come with her and was now amusing the company. Mother had always liked an entertainer.

The pain in my head was suddenly unendurable, and I climbed awkwardly off the bench hoping to make my way from the party unnoticed. Halfway around the house I heard my name and faltered and turned to find Madge hurrying behind me.

"Anny? Anny, are you sick or something?"

Surprised by her concern, I gulped and nodded. "Headache," I managed to mumble.

"Gee, that's a shame. Come in the house and I'll get you an aspirin."

"No," I said on a scratchy, outgoing breath. "I better go home. Don't say anyth—"

"Don't be a stupe," she interrupted. "Come on with me."

I thought I'd probably be better off at home, but it was balm to find someone caring about me, so I followed her meekly up the front porch, along the hall to a lavatory under the stairs.

"Here," she said, handing me two aspirins and a glass of water. "Take these. And then go on the front porch and rest for a while. You'll feel better in a bit. I thought you were acting awfully funny, but if you have a headache, that explains it."

"What do you mean, if?" I began, and then broke off.

123

Some calculating part of me warned that if here was a second chance to reach Madge—and so perhaps a chance to have friends at school—I'd better take it. Michael and maturity were a long way off, and seemed to be getting farther, not nearer. I had all these years of school to face while the growing-up process worked within me. Mother and I were not the same. Something had changed between us, and how could I tell if it would ever be undone, or we the same? Books seemed lost to me. And if I did not have Michael or Mother or books, what in the world did I have? What indeed? I said to myself on a spent and weary note. I wanted to lose myself in loss, exhaust myself with grief, but some stubborn core of resistance told me I might be glad of Madge's sponsorship one day and had better not spurn it now.

Since I couldn't stand deliberate calculation, I decided I'd liked her all along but just hadn't known it until this evening, and once I'd decided that was surprised to find that after all I did, in a way, like her. If only for being my own age.

For a moment, weakened by the clashing emotions of a too-long day, I wanted to tell her everything. All I felt, wanted, dreamed, suffered . . . everything I was and wanted to be. As if she were my sister. Or a best friend. Girls who were best friends did do that, I knew. They told each other things they'd never dream of telling parents, and I thought it must be rather wonderful.

Wavering, I realized it was impossible. Perhaps I'd spent too many years using books as a substitute for friends, repressing things too intricate and intimate to go into words. I looked at Madge and knew that we would never share our inner selves. There was something in her expression—some younger likeness to Maureen's expression of ruthless self-absorption and discontent, that made me shy away from wanting to know her inner being. But that's no reason, I decided, why we shouldn't share our outer ones. Sharing of any kind seemed welcome to me at that moment.

"You're awfully kind," I said clumsily.

"Think nothing of it. Say, I suspect Maureen's got ideas of moving in on your playwright. She thinks he's distinguished. He's got a bit of age on him, after all, doesn't he? Twenty-five, or something?"

"I . . . I think twenty-three."

"I guess I'll concentrate on something more in my class. Something easy. Say eleven or twelve. I have that defeated feeling that comes from being ignored, don't you? I don't think Maureen will get anywhere with him, either. She talks too much. All the Thaxters talk too much, for that matter."

"I know," I said, not thinking.

Madge wasn't put out. "Isn't Daddy *awful*? He says it's uncivilized not to have drink with dinner, but when Daddy gets into the bourbon he's about as civilized as Genghis Khan. He always gets mad at Maureen and me and goes on like that about the age of this and the generation of that. Terrible. No taste. Michael seems to hold his own, though. Come to think of it, he's quite a talker himself, which is why I don't think Maureen can make the grade with him. Talkers need listeners, don't you think?"

"Yes, I do." I closed my eyes and swayed a little.

"Sorry," said Madge. "Forgot about your head. Come on

out here on the porch, why don't you, and lay down—lie down—I always get mixed up with that, don't you? If you repose yourself here for a bit," she giggled, "you'll feel okay, I should think. Don't you?"

I nodded, swallowing hard. Did people—even talkative people—always talk as much as people seemed to be talking today? Even Michael was too much. On and on and on. I lay back in the low porch chair, gripping the arms with tense fingers, willing her to leave me alone. What a sad sorceress I'd have made, I thought irritably. Nobody reacts to my subliminal suggestions.

Madge, go away, I directed her with silent intensity. *You don't know why, Madge, but you are suddenly impelled to join the revelers in your back yard . . . Go!*

She pulled a chair close to mine and sat down.

"Honestly, Anny, what's he like? Has it been fun having him? Are you fond of him? Is he staying much longer? What's his play like? Have you seen it?"

I really began to feel as if something—Fate, in the form of a terrier—had me by the neck and was shaking the life out of me. And am I, I wondered, to be shaken limp and lifeless without a move to protect myself? I struggled to sit upright, found I couldn't because of the angle of the chair, and tried to look self-assertive from where I was. "Madge, don't misunderstand, but I honestly do have this headache. If I could just sit here for a bit, maybe . . ."

"Oh, sure, sure." She got to her feet, somewhat put out, somewhat sympathetic, tall and superior in her good health and spirits. "You coming back when you feel better?"

She was taking a lot of trouble over me, and I was grateful. "Of course," I said. "In just a little while."

At last she was gone.

Thy sweet child, Sleep, the filmy eyed, murmured like a noontide bee wouldst thou me? And I replied, No, not thee—

There was always some poem, some adage, some errant line of prose in my mind. These words came easily enough as I looked into the drowsy darkness of the Thaxters' vast front lawn. Somebody or other's law says that two things cannot occupy the same space at the same time, and I find this is true enough of the mind. To say an ode of Shelley's through is all a mortal mind can do . . . it can't be asked for thinking, too. I occupied myself in this way, and then tried to remember the poem from the beginning—

Swiftly walk o'er the western wave, spirit of night. Out of the misty eastern cave where all the long and lone daylight thou wovest dreams of joy and fear, which make thee—

But to be successful in this kind of evasion you are obliged to be on guard every second, to keep your mind sternly on the words, or without knowing it you stop reciting and begin thinking again. I was not vigilant enough, and somewhere in the very first stanza my attention went from Shelley to Michael. Once again I found myself, grown and desirable, standing in a hotel lobby in Boston—or Bombay—waiting for the door to open and Michael to appear, his eyes searching, finding me, hesitating—

"Michael, I'm not at all sure this is what we should be doing."

127

That was my mother's voice somewhere on the lawn. It was difficult to tell whether near or far. I sat, helpless as if impaled, in the shadows of the porch, and listened.

"It won't be for long," he said, his voice strangely young and pleading.

"But there's a perfectly good company of people back there, and I'm enjoying the party. If there's something you especially want to say—" She waited, and I waited, but there was nothing. Only the fiddle sound of crickets rising from the grass, only the swell of music and laughter from the back yard. Only the sound of my own heart, beating, beating.

"Well," Mother said, as if relenting, "perhaps it *is* nice to be away from the clamor for a bit. Lordy . . . I'm stuffed. Mr. Thaxter can't get his steaks from a regular butcher. *Where* do you suppose he gets them?"

"From a bank, maybe?"

Mother laughed, but I had detected a note of wistfulness in Michael's voice. Couldn't she hear it? Could only I, who loved him, know the subtle changes that spelled his moods? She seemed terribly insensitive. Only . . . why should she be sensitive where Michael was concerned? He was only that self-absorbed young man to her, someone she perhaps liked a little but who meant nothing real to her.

I wondered if I should cough or call out or put my hands over my ears. I did nothing and was not even sure they hadn't walked softly over the grass and away, back to the party. But in a little while Mother said, in an indulgent but faintly impatient way (I knew the tones of her voice, too), "*Was* there something, Michael?"

"I . . . I don't know."

128

"I see. Well . . ." There was another silence, and then she said, "Do you know anything about astronomy, about stars?"

"Nothing more abstruse than the Big Dipper and the evening star. Mrs. Miles—"

"Not where Ursa is?" my mother interrupted. "The Bear? A friend of mine used to say he liked the Bear. For myself, I like all the stars, but I can't tell one from the other. Funny thing, when you come to think of it, going around saying you like the Bear."

"Yes, it is, isn't it?" How flat, how unlike him, was his voice. "I know why you interrupted me just then," he began.

"Possibly," said Mother. "Tell me, you're a chemist, no?"

"Yes."

"An alchemist, yes?"

"No."

"Fiddle around with elixirs and philtres and potions?"

"Yes and no," he said with a short laugh.

I did not like my mother at the moment. If Michael wanted to speak, she should let him speak, whether she wanted to get back to the party or not. I didn't know how she could want to leave the bliss of Michael's sole presence for any reason at all, but admitted that since she was not I it was possible. Only, if he needed to be listened to—

Oh, if only he'd come to me, I thought. If only he'd come to me—

"Then give me a recipe for heartache," Mother said. "Some old simple from the witch in the wood. You know."

There was a long, long pause, and then Michael said,

"Well, let's see . . . there's henbane, and hemp . . . and hemlock, hellebore, dittany, and mulberry. And there's mandrake and lettuce—" His fascination with words asserted itself, and he began to sound less a wretched wight palely loitering around a belle dame who had no mercy anyway for him, and more like a chemist whose main interest was writing.

It's like giving candy to a child for distraction, I thought, glad he was distracted and vexed with Mother for finding him so maneuverable.

"My, you do have them all at your fingertips," she said, before his list was exhausted. "I suppose I could start with lettuce. Does it have to be picked in the moonlight and accompanied by some sort of dance?"

"Mrs. Miles—" he began, stopped, went on quaveringly. "Please, couldn't I call you Nan?"

"Fair enough, I guess. I call you Michael. Though the difference in our ages—"

"Oh, *damn* the difference in our ages. Do you think that really matters?"

"I don't think about it one way or the other. I was only saying—"

"But let *me* say, instead. Nan, if your heart aches—"

"What are you talking about? My heart doesn't ache. And if it did, I wouldn't be confiding in—that is, I would be apt to keep it to myself. I think we'd better go back."

It was not fair of her to act surprised. What else could he have taken her words to mean?

"What do you mean, what do I mean?" Michael said, sounding for the first time like a man and not a pleading boy. "You ask for a heartache remedy, and I give you a dozen specifics and then offer a better one—or try to—and you ask what I'm talking about. What have you been talking about?"

"I'm sorry," she said. "I'm really very sorry. I wasn't thinking about myself at all. I was thinking about—"

I had a sudden chilled apprehension. Was it for me she'd sought a list of simples for the relief of a hurting heart? Mother, don't you do this to me, I shrieked silently, and in a moment would have leaped from my place in the shadows, indifferent to their reaction, just so I stopped her tongue.

Either my cry reached her, or wasn't necessary, because she said, "Look here, Michael, if I've misled you, I'm sorry. I seem to have been speaking at random, and the truth is, I really didn't mean a thing at all. Or, if I did, I spoke unwisely and now wish to take it all back, if you will be so good as to allow me. Surely you've allowed your tongue to wander at times, and then realized you should have kept still?" He said nothing, and in a moment she went on, "Well, I think you have. Everyone does it. Only everyone is not as lucky as me, having a person like you, who will listen and understand . . ."

"You needn't lay it on any more," he said tiredly. "I get the message. I get all of them. Everything you're trying to tell me."

"I'm sorry," she said again.

"You aren't, really. But that's all right." He exhaled in a long, audible sigh. "I'm going to go and pack. I'll get the morning train out of here, and—well, make my excuses to the Thaxters, will you?"

"All right."

"Is that all you have to say?"

"I don't know what else to say."

131

"You don't really care at all, do you? Whether I go or stay, or when, or how I feel or anything?"

"I care—" she began.

He interrupted angrily, "No, you *don't*."

"Well . . . then I don't."

"Forgive me, forgive me," he mumbled. "I don't seem to know what I'm saying. I thought I did. I knew what I wanted to say. I've been thinking about it all evening, planning how to put it—"

"You didn't mean it," she said gently.

"Don't interpret for me, please."

But now he was not angry, only sad sounding, and very tired. My heart beat heavily for him. And for myself, too, I thought. For myself.

It's funny, I thought, that I didn't guess. The way he makes excuses to talk about her, the way he notices all her moods and changes, and hangs around watching her, and shows off when she's present. Now it was so plain to me, the way pleasure leaped in his eyes at her laughter and her off-hand humor, her pretty, inconsequential sayings, her sound delight in each day's recurrence. I saw now how that pleasure had drained away when she fell, headlong as it seemed, into grief.

I supposed he had hoped to comfort and sustain her, to draw her love to him now that its other object was gone. I could have told him, I thought, that plain love of living is what will comfort Mother. It always has.

I wondered what to do now. Michael, in speaking, and I, in eavesdropping, had altered, finally and completely, the world that for me had been shifting and changing shape all sum-

132

mer. There would never be a way back to the place where my mother was my mother alone and not a person of her own, to where dreams of love were truer than love itself, and make-believe was not the refuge but the reality. Even before Michael came I had begun to know that books and Mother did not comprise the world, that I could dig in my heels and go deaf and become a pillar of dumb protest, but that if I would not go to life, it would come to me. The collision had been inevitable.

I didn't notice when they left, whether separately or together, in peace or in conflict. They had—for now—nothing to do with me. I had only to do with myself.

"I don't care," I said to myself. "I don't care what happens. I'll show them."

With the old childish threat on my lips, I set out to journey over a strange new landscape from which the mists seemed to be clearing only enough to disclose its crags and precipices.

CHAPTER NINE

On the evening of my twentieth birthday I was dressing for a date with Jeff when the phone rang in the hall and someone shouted, "Anny Miles! Boston calling."

Pulling on my robe, I ran out and took up the receiver.

"Darling, happy birthday," Mother said. "Did you get our present? Are you going to have any fun for the occasion? Why aren't you out somewhere? I didn't actually expect to find you in—"

"Mrs. *Sher*wood!" I said, laughing. "You go too fast for me. Yes, I got them, I adore them, I'm wearing them tonight." Mother and Peter had sent me filigree gold earrings with little pendent jade drops. "They're beautiful, Mother, and I thank you both. I'll write a note, but anyway, tell Peter. And I'm here because I'm getting dressed. We keep later than New England hours down here."

"Of course, Anny. I keep forgetting. Where are you going? Who with?"

134

"The theater and supper. With Jeff Roland."

"Oh? Jeff again? How *nice*, Anny." She put much significance into the words, and I laughed again. "Do I sound like *I, Madame Matrimonial Director?*" Mother asked.

"Somewhat."

"Well, I didn't really *mean* anything. I just thought—" She waited, and I didn't help her out, so after a moment she said, "Anyway, do have a marvelous time for your birthday. How's school?"

"Wonderful, Mother. Wonderful. You won't believe all I'm learning."

I was going to a woman's college just outside New York City. It was owing to Mother's husband, Peter Sherwood, that I'd gotten to college at all, and every morning when I woke I thought, It's true, it's true. I'm really here. And then I'd think, *Bless Peter.*

"I'd believe anything of you," Mother said now, and then went on to tell me what she and Peter were doing. "Did you hear from Lenore?" she asked suddenly.

"I did. She sent me a birthday card." I hesitated, went on reluctantly, "She wrote on the back of it that Mr. Beard died."

"Oh, Anny! Oh, I'm sorry. But what a peculiar thing for her to do. I mean, what an odd way to tell you."

"Nothing's odd that Lenore does," I said wryly.

A few minutes later, in my room again, I made a motion to continue dressing, and then sat down and stared out the window. Plundering autumn was at the trees, wresting from the branches leaves gold and brown, yellow and scarlet, coasting them along the wind and over the campus grounds in parrot-bright profusion. I looked intently, carefully, at the old administration building, the aged and ivy-walled science building, the mettlesome, modern auditorium with its abstract-expressionist air. There were boxwood hedges and lawns of cropped grass and gardens showy with asters and chrysanthemums and little flaming marigolds. These grounds and buildings were my world now. Within them I was learning all that brilliance and patience and devotion could teach me.

Bless Peter, I thought again, and still did not move.

Mr. Beard was dead. Gone, like Tabu, to the next world, or to nothing. I still did not know what I thought lay beyond that last breath, that last flash of vision. But Mr. Beard lying in Kittery forever, and Tabu forever in the secret place at the end of the garden had not gone to nothing for me. Part of me, always. And alive.

But how long, how long ago, that other autumn and Mother and me flying from pain in opposite directions—

For relief from grief, people go to gardens, to books, to church, to other lands, and since grief is a passion that can be assuaged only by another passion, they turn to these things utterly, losing themselves in flowers, words, God, exotic places.

It was my mother's way to go to other people. She had forgotten for a time, but now turned back to them, and, lacking Mr. Wade, gave Mr. Beard and Mrs. Halley and me the full benefit of her devotion.

Mrs. Halley thawed and almost grew gentle under the ravishing warmth of Mother's consideration. Mr. Beard was heard to whistle on his little evening strolls. Cousin Jim

136

Northrup came to dinner one night and was so sweetly welcomed (even I, through inattention, overlooked his sloppy appearance) that he began to be a regular weekly guest. In December he brought an engineer, a big dreamy man named Peter Sherwood, who'd been a widower for several years, to visit. In January Mr. Sherwood rented the attic room, though he was away more often than he was with us. He seemed to come out of his dreams when Mother was around.

So they all profited from her way of escaping the hurt and the memory of lost love.

And I? My flight from grief threw me into high school, a place that until then I had considered for learning only. I traveled light in my new world, leaving behind me all that made the other world enchanted. Michael, Mother, Tabu, Sydney Carton, all my books. With Madge for a wedge, or a shield, I gained entrance to her branch of high-school society and there carefully followed the pattern, the figures stylized as a minuet, though the beat was rock and roll and nothing stately.

Mother was happy for me at first. She liked my having a "crowd." She liked providing food we could ill afford for a gang of young barbarians who ate and ran. Her eyes sparkled as she saw me off to dances, or basketball games, or slumber parties, and she said, "Hush" to Lenore, who complained that I never lifted a finger any more.

"She's never had this," I heard her tell Lenore.

"And what *is* this may I ask?" said Lenore, actually waiting to hear the answer.

"You must know, Lenore. The fun of being with people her own age. Of being part of a group. Of being a normal, thoughtless adolescent, not an overworked child who reads too much."

"She was better off and a nicer person the other way," said this strangely terse Lenore.

I listened, and snapped my fingers and ran off, not caring what they thought. They had nothing to do with me, nor I with them.

Michael sent me the works of the Brontë sisters, bound in pale green leather. I put the books away after a brief glance and said to Mother, "Those Vyes have a way of sending one last token before they disappear into eternal silence, don't they?"

Mother hesitated, and then said, "There's no reason why Michael should disappear. For you, I mean. There's no reason why someday—"

"Oh, Mother," I broke in. "Please. I couldn't care less."

I thought I couldn't. When I remembered him, it was not with longing but a dull sense of having been duped. He had, I decided, made a fool of me, and besides that had estranged me from my mother. I blamed him for the hectic, restless, unsatisfied route I was traveling now.

For the truth was, I did not like being part of a "crowd." I found the pattern pointless, the conversation without meaning, the people of my own age alien, where Mr. Beard, who was not too old for me, and Michael, who was, had seemed familiar and real, if not always understandable, and where my mother, who was ageless, had made a focal point for everything.

Fall went by, and winter, and in the early spring I climbed one day to my room and the window seat, welcomed Tabu, whom sometimes I forgot for days, and said to myself, "I must think what this is all about."

Out of a sense of—what? Rejection, revenge, outrage?—I had streaked off toward a new way of life, thinking to be independent and grown up, no longer reliant on the old supports, a person fully acceptable to her peer group, indifferent to all others, achieving maturity with my contemporaries.

Mother and Lenore did their own work, and mine, and began to show the signs. Lenore was quarrelsome where she had only been querulous. Mother was still in radiant humor, but too tired at night for a movie, or a walk, or a game of cards. She went to bed earlier and earlier, and did me the favor of not appearing to stay awake until I got in. I was not sure if she did or not. Tabu was growing thin, and now that I thought of it, I hadn't heard her purr in weeks. Mrs. Halley never asked me to run errands any more or join her in a game of solitaire, and Mr. Beard looked at me as if I were a broken promise.

And what was the nature of the brave new world that I'd left my other world to conquer or, anyway, live in?

Well, I didn't know what age fifteen to sixteen was for some in that school—possibly real and full of value. I judged only by my piece of the puzzle, the jigsawed particles that Madge had offered me to play with, and there I could fit nothing to anything. The passwords, the high signs, were now familiar to me, except that I didn't know their meaning. The giggles and the gossip and the casual cruelties enmeshed me. I smoked in secret, sometimes drank, once got drunk, and once kissed a boy I didn't know. For the first time in my life

139

I failed a subject and even convinced myself that I didn't care.

One day I said to Madge, "Does all this really strike you as fun, as what you want from life?"

"How do I know what I want from life?" she said. "I know what I'm getting, and I have to make do with that, don't I?"

"I don't see why. It seems to me that you examine what you have, and then if it doesn't suit, you try something else. At least, that's what it seems to me," I repeated, being somewhat timid in my provisional membership in this club, not ready yet to give it up.

"This is what comes of being nice to people who can't make the grade on their own. I actually only took you on at all because I was sorry for you."

Madge, as I had noted before, suffered from a limited vocabulary. She seemed, more and more, to suffer graver limitations than that, and as time went on I began to be panicked, wondering if through my new-found fear of ostracism I would grow to be just like her, making do with what I had, no matter how meaningless and vile, because it was all I knew.

But it isn't all I know, I told myself now, clutching Tabu to me, so that she wriggled in protest and sprang away. I have known poetry and friendship and love. I have known kindness and curiosity, and great books, and pity. Mother thinks that I'm frolicking normally with young people at last, and she is happy. She's too innocent to see that these young people are having a dance with the devil and will dance it at any cost.

I leaned back, motionless, the room darkening as dusk came on, and thought, I won't go on with this dance. I have to get out of it, and breathe again, and see the people I know.

140

I leaped from the window seat and ran through the house and out to the garden, looking for my mother.

She was stooping down, examining some flower shoots in the border by the house. "Think of it, Anny," she said, not turning. "The daffodils are starting up already."

I settled beside her and looked at the tiny green beaks thrusting upward.

"So they are," I said. A sense of peace and homecoming pulsed in my veins. "Spring is coming, after all."

"Did you think it wouldn't?" she said with a gentle smile.

"For a while I wasn't quite sure."

That was all. I never did explain to her my sudden return to scholarship and books and Mr. Beard, to my duties as the landlady's daughter, and my trips to the library for Mrs. Halley—and myself. I never said why I wanted to be with her again, after months of pretending I didn't have a mother at all, since, in the circles I frequented, parents were infra dig.

And she never asked. Innocent she may have been, but she missed little of what went on in our town, or in life.

"It's about time you pulled yourself together your poor mother was worried sick let me tell you running around with that fast crowd like you were and failing in school and acting like a kid all of a sudden—"

"All of a sudden?" I interrupted Lenore. "What does that mean?"

"It means you were a pretty sensible person until you got in with that bunch of half-crazy thrill-seekers."

"I certainly never noticed that you considered me a sensible person."

"I guess you had to act like a fool for me to know you weren't one," she grumbled.

141

"If you and Mother knew what that bunch were like, why didn't you stop me?" I asked coldly.

"Many's the time I wanted to say something believe you me but your mother from the day you were born has given you credit for common sense and she said you couldn't be talked into something you had to find out for yourself that high heels and highballs don't make a grownup—oh, never fear," she said at my expression, "we knew that time you got tight and your mother was beside herself only she said Lenore it won't do any good to lecture at her and carry on she's sound and good and she'll find out for herself God grant I said that she'll find out before she does something that can't be undone it's a chance we have to take she said but she looked terrible and Mr. Sherwood wanted to put your hat on straight believe you me but she wouldn't hear of it—"

"Mr. Sherwood? What does he have to do with me, or anything?"

"Well just because you're past noticing what goes on in your own home don't mean nothing goes on Miss High-and-Mighty and for your information Mr. Sherwood cares for your mother."

"Cares for her?" I sounded stupid, but I'd hardly taken cognizance of Mr. Sherwood. To have him presented as a carer for my mother was dumfounding. "What about Mr. Wade?"

"Huh what about him indeed your mother's a lovely attractive woman and can't be expected to sit mooning over the silverneers of people that don't care for her—"

"He did," I interrupted. "I don't know anything about Mr. Sherwood, but Mr. Wade was in love with Mother."

142

"So that's over and done with she grieved enough and I'm glad to see how she's coming around laughing and thinking about new clothes—"

But I'd heard enough. "I have to do my homework," I said, and left Lenore talking. She and I were as rude with each other as a pair of pups in a litter and continue so to this day, when we meet.

At my desk I pulled a notebook and geometry text toward me and settled to work, but in a little while put down the pencil to stare across the room.

"So now it's Mr. Sherwood?" I said to myself, and waited, expecting that rise of protest and jealousy, that former rebellious sense of Mother's wrongly usurping what should be my place. I was sixteen, and therefore might well have admirers. The fact that I did not should be beside the point. The point, surely, was that Mother should have had enough by now.

I doodled a cat on the notebook, preparing to cope with dissension, but it failed to come. Instead, I found myself shaking my head with a sort of baffled indulgence. The way, in a town this size, she managed to gather admirers was a wonder, and I was coming to the conclusion that, consciously or not, my mother was a flirt. I'd been reading about flirts all my life, from Circe through Becky Sharp to Amber, and I knew one thing—you could as soon expect one to stop aging as stop flirting, and the one had apparently no effect on the other. Look at Ninon de Lenclos. Or George Sand.

But then Michael wasn't at fault anywhere. Men who hear the siren song and can't resist are not culpable. And, I thought, if the siren is unaware of her song's enchantment, if she thinks she's just singing to herself while she sorts the linen and shucks the corn, then she is blameless, too. And for last summer's turbulence and internecine strife I surely couldn't blame myself. When Sydney Carton and Rhett Butler threatened to go back in the books and never come forth again, I looked up from the pages and saw Michael and fell in love with him. Natural, inescapable.

We had all behaved as we had to behave and time had borne us along from last summer to now when we could no longer entirely remember what we were or wanted then. Except that I could feel, like a small warm spark, love for Michael lifting in me once again—a renouncing love for a Michael of the past. And I realized now that I would never seek him in the future.

> *Because I know that time is always time*
> *And place is always and only place*
> *And what is actual is actual only for one time*
> *And only for one place*
> *I rejoice that things are as they are—*

I could not recall the rest of the lines, except that somewhere in them occurred the words, *These matters that with myself I too much discuss, too much explain—*

"Enough!" I said to myself. Last summer, today, it's all part of what I thought would never happen and what is happening all the time. One grows up, one grows up . . . and it would be good, for a while, just to take it on faith.

I finished up the geometry, and went downstairs to set the table for dinner. For the first time in months I passed

144

the attic door without the bitter glance that had become almost automatic, almost without meaning. I didn't know what it was I wanted. But not, anyway, a ghost behind closed doors. It was something out in the world.

Time, which for me was still flexible and still endless-seeming, was not so for Mr. Peter Sherwood. He moved into the house in January, courted Mother until April, and married her in May. We moved to Boston, and Lenore, who'd been more provident by far than Mother, bought our house, painted the yellow clapboard white, partitioned the attic, and ended up with six boarders, including Cousin Jim.

Mother was very happy. Peter is one of the good men of the world, one of the strong men. I don't know how often Mrs. Sherwood thought of Mr. Wade. I suppose it was seldom. My mother is a realist, very sure that what is actual is actual only for one time. I'm a romantic, and don't quite believe it. I tended to remember Mr. Wade a good deal in the beginning. I would wonder how he was, what his days held, what his future would be. I always seemed to remember him arriving in a blizzard, laughing as he stomped the snow off his boots and held out this Saturday's package for Mother to open. But in time that image faded, and the recollection of him, and I expect one day his slight shadow will slip entirely beyond my recall.

When we'd been in Boston a year, Tabu died of a fever. I took her back home and buried her in that place at the end of the garden where, long after I had ceased to visit it, she used to go to recover from the fatigues of her futile hunting. She's the only cat I ever knew who couldn't catch a bird, and I still think she didn't really mean to. I left her for the last time and wandered back between the flourishing bean rows, thinking of her, of Michael, of that morning of wild promise. . . .

Lenore met me at the back door. "Well are you all done what a lot of morbid nonsense come on in and sit with me while I do these jellies how's your mother I never hear a peep out of either of you well maybe she writes but you certainly don't you'd think I hadn't practically brought you up—"

And I'd think right, I said to myself, but sat, for courtesy and old time's sake, a little while before I went where I wanted to go, out on the front porch to Mr. Beard.

He was very frail now, more tremorous and less woeful.

"Have you seen that Echo?" he asked me.

"The satellite? Lots of times, going across Boston."

He smiled a little. "That's a nice way you put it . . . going across Boston. Goes across Kittery, too. And here. And Bombay, India. And Siberia. Does it look to you like it wavers a little?"

"Yes, it does."

"Not as steady as a star, you see. A man-made star, with a little man-made waver in it. But it's beautiful. I'm always glad I lived to see it."

"But I thought you didn't approve of people in space, Mr. Beard."

"Well, and I didn't. But I don't know, Anny. That Echo makes me think. You'd think if man could work a wonder like that, maybe he can work the real wonder, and find peace. Maybe sailing around in the skies will give him perspective."

"We can hope so," I said.

"Yes." He sighed deeply. "Yes, that's what we'd better

146

hope." He sat, holding between the palms of his hands the pipe that he didn't smoke any more, looking with his old eyes at the evening sky.

"Mr. Beard, *thank you,*" I said on impulse.

"Thank you, Anny? Thank me for what?"

It would take too long, it would be too hard to explain. "Just thank you," I said.

"Well, you're very welcome, Anny," he said, and nodded at me.

The next year I came here to study, to learn, to grow and grow older, carried inexorably from moment to moment by Time, which was not man-made and never wavered.

One rainy April evening this year I was in town, buying socks, and was hurrying to meet a teacher who'd said she'd drive me back in her car, when I ran full tilt into a man as he charged around a corner.

"Oh, lordy," I said. "Sorry." I snatched at my package to keep it from falling into a puddle and then, rather wildly, wishing he'd get out of the way, glanced up. In the spattered, windy light of a street lamp, I saw his face, and breathed to myself, *Michael . . . Oh, Michael, my love—*

But it was a trick of the light in the night and the rain. It was not Michael, come to me since I was grown and had not gone to him. It was Jeff.

The poet says, *I am a part of all that I have met,* and I think this must be true. But I believe, too, that the person you love is a part of all you've met. That's why Jeff, whom I love very much and will marry when he asks me—he will ask me—is partly Michael Vye of my fifteenth summer and my

147

first love. Though Jeff is all perception and understanding, I do not think I will ever say to him that I'm not sure if I've loved one man twice or two men once.

It doesn't matter. I've known more than Michael Vye in my life, and Jeff is the sum of these parts. He is compounded of his own dear self, and of Michael, and my mother, and of Mr. Beard. I hear my father in his voice sometimes, and Mr. Wade in his laugh. I see Sydney Carton in his eyes. I see Tabu there, too, the tamed and untamable.

Jeff is both a part and the sum of all that I have met, and —if it so please Providence—of all that I shall ever meet again.

MARY STOLZ was born in Boston, Massachusetts, and grew up in New York City. An avid reader since childhood, Mrs. Stolz cannot remember when she first began to write. TO TELL YOUR LOVE, her first book for young people, was published in 1950. Since then she has written the many novels which have established her reputation as one of America's finest writers for teen-agers.

Among Mrs. Stolz's many popular books are SOME MERRY-GO-ROUND MUSIC, SECOND NATURE, AND LOVE REPLIED, and THE BEAUTIFUL FRIEND.

1961